Black Velvet

First published by Brandon D. Fuller at Smashwords.com

Stoneprismsmedia@gmail.com

Chapter List

Ch.1: Johnny Velvet

February nights in Dallas can be eerily frostbitten, a brutal cold after a warm day in the metroplex. Usually the city is absolved from the snowy months of the east coast and Midwest, but sheets of ice are left as a trail of evidence marking winter's passing through. Each of the roads present a unique challenge, if they are to be navigated without much incident. In life though, no such roads seem to exist. Ironically, it would be the same roads, covered in hazardous black ice, that would claim the lives of both Scarlet Velvet and Joseph Turner, leaving their son Johnny to navigate the same treacherous roads alone.

Called Vel by his grandparents and peers, at 19 years old, it has been ten entire years since the tragic accident that killed his parents. Every year February presents a difficult time for Vel, who use to be painstakingly resigned to complete silence for the entire month up until his sixteenth birthday. That year, his grandparents invested in something that would snap him fully out of his depression, and into a life of blazing confidence, and even greater speeds!

That was Vel's first motorbike, a pieced together Kawasaki with it's fuel tank painted lime green and the fender powder blue. His first task would be repainting the oddly colored fender, "a cool Dallas Cowboy blue". Although he can hear his grandmother's voice like it was yesterday saying, "you mean navy," correcting him in jest, the bike he would give the name "Einstein," would become Vel's single most endearing fascination. That fascination would slowly grow problematic for his elderly guardians who had only sought to aid him in his time of need. First there were the rings of dirt formed in the back yard as a result of his falling and spinning in place, wiping out a huge portion of his grandmother's garden. Next was his unwittingly youthful attempt to ride the bike to school, sans license or permit. That one almost saw Vel face near expulsion, more so because of his bullheaded refusal to apologize than anything. He had gotten his stubbornness from his mother who was a former superintendent in the Dallas school system. Despite being born in the inner city, after the accident Vel would relocate from the harsh neighborhoods of the south side to Mansfield with his grandparents.

Vel never did receive that expulsion, only a moderate three day suspension meant to prove a point. To the street racing scene though, and boys much older, he had already proven a point of his own, that he was not only willing to bend the rules, but to reshape them altogether according to his mind's will. Albeit it was a mind that prioritized engines over school principles. Now all he had to do was make it to graduation. Ben Barber Academy was a notoriously strict institution as is, and it seemed that it would take an act of God for him to remain there uninhibited moving forward. As delicate as she was stern and quick witted would arrive such blessing in disguise, packaged in a 24-year-old student counselor by the name of Jessica Hillsbury. Of course she was the youngest amongst all counselors, as well as a target to some, but she was the daughter of a United States District Attorney. Not that she needed it to keep Vel's attention, to him Ms. Hillsbury was inconceivably flawless. For the maturing sixteen year old, sticking around another two years was an easy decision, if it meant that he would get to talk with her every day. Besides, his grandparents would probably kill him together.

Senior year was pretty much a breeze, going by faster with each passing day. That is, until the night of Ben Barber's Prom, which Vel had opted to skip despite the urging from from his grandmother. The night before she would visit his room upstairs as he prepared himself for bed. She insisted that his mind could be changed if he had known more, about what prom had meant to his own mother.

"You know, prom night was everything to your mother," she revealed before finishing, "she was even voted Prom Queen!"

Even with such explanation Vel maintains an uninterested position explaining nonchalantly, "grandma, all girls like prom." Abruptly after he finishes speaking, his grandmother withdraws a small crown and hands it to him. "That was her tiara from that night," she reveals before turning and heading for the bedroom exit.

She tells him, "it was a crown fit for a mother to be," then leaves the room, shutting the door behind her.

Yes, his grandma Thelma had indeed left him with a treasure older than he was in his mother's tiara, but her last words were nearly just as meaningful, if not more. Much more than dates and dances, it had been prom night that his mother had told grandma Thelma, about her pregnancy. Vel's conception was hidden to everyone, even his father Joseph. Slowly her words began to set in, drawing him to her bedside at once. "Grandma, do you think my old man would approve of this suit?" asks Vel, watching as Grandma Thelma's giant smile seemingly illuminates the room. If anything was worthwhile, it was that alone. Afterwards she went on to inform him how, "Joseph Turner was the finest dressed boy in the whole city!" That was a huge compliment coming from Grandma

Thelma, considering her infamous disdain of him. She once chased him off of her lawn with a pair of lawn sheers threatening to cut his head off! Vel was nearly three years old before his mother built up the courage to return home, the first time Grandma Thelma laid eyes on him. Those were tough days for the family at the time, but I guess reflecting on them, and considering things to come, they are rather amusing.

The next night Grandma Thelma would present Vel with the dazzling velvet suit that his father had wore, matching his mother's radiant velvet dress. Even Grandpa Charles and Bo had decided to get in on the evening's celebration, showering him with barbeque and soggy dog kisses! As Vel pulled Einstein around to the front of the house from the shed, the three of them awaited eagerly on the porch, more giddy than Vel himself. The old bike makes a crackling noise before starting, causing Grandma Thelma's excitement to immediately turn into worry.

She offers, "are you sure you don't want me and Charles to drop you off tonight?"

As soon as she finishes Bo gives a loud snapping bark, almost defiantly.

"Oh and Bo," she quickly adds.

In an instant Vel starts the bike, which sputters momentarily, and is off down the road. About three miles along however, he pulls into a grouping of trees and turns off the bike. Out of his backpack he withdraws some jeans, a T-shirt, and his street racing helmet. After changing he neatly folds up the velvet suit, staring at it briefly, then places it inside of his bag. He jumps back onto Einstein and hits the open road with a vengeance. Although that night had been destined as prom night for most of Mansfield, for a select few high schoolers from the area it was the night of the big underground gum ball rally. The rally was designed to move along a route that shot straight through the heart of downtown Mansfield, and into an area known as The Dust, at dangerously high speeds! Einstein roars loudly as it pulls up to the rally starting point, to the amusement of a few students who each chuckle at Vel's old model bike. One of the older looking boys, a Kurt Cobain carbon copy, or knockoff, declares, "too bad I didn't bring my grandpa, or you two would've really given each other a good challenge!" His group of about six flunkies each burst into uncontrollable laughter as if it was the first good joke they had ever heard.

"Enough!" he yells, causing each of them to instantly turn pale in silence.

"Jesus Christ Chayne it's our Prom night!" cries a teenage girl seated behind him, apparently his date, or girlfriend. After revving the motor of his fancy motorbike he smirks at Vel then announces to his date, "don't worry sweetheart, I'm going to win this quick enough that we won't miss a thing."

From atop a bridge nearby, the flag bearers and crowd of spectators all stand ready as no less than thirteen vehicles each make their way to the starting line. Three of them are seniors from the high school football team, but the rest have traveled from various cities to take place in the big race. The driver of a souped up Baja Trophy Truck approaches the line and revs the truck's powerful engine in a effectively intimidating fashion. All eyes become glued to the mighty power display, except those of Chayne in his Ford Focus Rs Rx, Vel, and two long haired, steely eyed brothers, both whom drove mean looking ATV Buggies. One of the flag bearers screams, "racers ready!" The others wave their flags and everyone takes off!

Through the first straightaway that presents itself Vel finds himself pushing Einstein full throttle, only to be claiming a stake in no greater than eighth place. He spends the next few minutes blocked behind most of his competitors who almost seem to be working together to take Vel out! They swerve recklessly in front of him in a criss crossing pattern, one of the dirty drivers yelling, "tactics boy, aren't you still supposed to be in preschool!?" Everyone looks well experienced at these rallies, and wasted no time in pointing out and taking advantage of Vel's youthful ignorance. These races weren't just friendly competition, and these drivers weren't school kids. If he was going to finish the race, or more importantly not get killed, then he was going to have to allow his natural instincts to take over, before it was too late.

The first winding curve would also be his first opportunity to prove that he could keep pace with this fierce class of drivers. Rally races are notorious for their battles against the terrain, and being so, the course had been designed to test their skills and wheels, at the exact moment. As he slightly bends going top speed, he sees a sea of brake lights, all cautious as the concrete has suddenly turned into a slick gravel! Vel's sudden slow in momentum nearly flips him from the bike, but he holds tight, shifting his weight to get realigned. This was his moment though, and he knew it, revving Einstein as powerfully as possible, exploding directly through the center of the traffic! The driver of the Baja truck slaps his steering wheel in frustration, resembling the two buggy driving brothers who exchange icy glares at each other as their younger counterpart rapidly passes by. Just ahead of Vel however remains the determined and altogether devastating Rs Rx driven by the boy known as Chayne. Seeing Vel appear in his rearview only serves to make him drive harder, perfectly executing the next couple of turns which make each of the other vehicles brake slightly. Einstein though continues to throttle relentlessly across the gravel and through each turn coming into the last straightaway.

This time each vehicle accelerates to top speed with the finishing point now in clear sight, only the group is not alone anymore. They've been joined by two police cruisers! Unfortunately the local sheriff was enjoying dinner parked along the last turn exiting The Dust, and he was furious. Not only that, he wasn't bad behind the wheel himself. At least five vehicles would come to a halt at the mere sight of the crazed sheriff moving with such calculated reckless abandon. Tickets would be given to each of them by the lone officer assisting the wild apprehension. The sheriff's eyes nevertheless were dead set on bringing the last two vehicles remaining to justice, Chayne and Vel.

Now both Vel and his ferocious competition had to decide which was going to be their top priority, evading the raging sheriff and escaping in one piece, or simply winning the race. It would be Chayne that would choose the latter, with Vel too being driven by the demented look in his eyes that saw victory as his only mission. How could he dare call himself a street racer, if he was unwilling to match his opponent's intensity and desire to close the deal? As if his veins were pumping high octane gasoline Vel again pushes Einstein to its limits in response! The explosion of power, causing flames to exit his exhaust, startles

Chayne for just a moment as he looks in his rearview. Vel though has shot past him, but not for long.

"Chayne Chambers stop your vehicle now! You are in the act of a felony!" The sheriff has gone to the loud speaker, apparently with Chayne's full identity available to him. For those reasons, and the fact that Vel is an ineligible driver, paper tags adorn the back of Einstein. The booming sound of thunder, followed by immediate rain, forces Vel to a stop, with the finish line just ahead. When he looks back, he sees Chayne, who looks back at him in bitter defeat, then worry. This causes Vel to feel torn even more. Was he willing to let a fellow racer, a potential rival even, be captured and taken to jail if he could help it? As the rain picks up, the sheriff finally exits his vehicle, the dirt beneath him quickly turning into a sludgy mud. When Chayne sits back in his defeat, Vel sees something that makes him do the unthinkable. A boy, presumably his son, is sitting in the passenger seat, the ignorantly blissful risks of his father becoming his own. To that, Vel abruptly revs Einstein into gear and shoots in the sheriff and Chayne's direction! The sheriff of course is startled, attempting to withdraw his gun but drops it thanks to the rain. Only a few feet away Vel brings Einstein to a twisting stop, splashing mud all over the sheriff and his car! Although surprised, Chayne finally acknowledges the younger Vel, before revving his Ford and burning off. Vel smiles, happy to have competed with and received respect from the such a driver. His smile disappears altogether when his eyes meet with the fuming sheriff's, a man who from that moment on swore to have his vengeance, in the form of Johnny Velvet.

Ch.2: More Motors, More Problems

Everyone has that one thing that makes them tick, that gets their juices flowing and engines turning, passionately grinding the gears of their muse, in hopes of one day bearing the wonder filled fruits of such true happiness. Or at least, that's the way that it should be. Then again, life for most begins where such utopia ceases, and our vulnerabilities are exposed. Since he was sixteen, for Vel that one thing had been Einstein, his perfectly imperfect companion. No, Einstein didn't speak the language of people, the bike had spoken to Vel's spirit, soothing the boy's constant yearning to be free from the shackles of his own life. In each of the bike's parts, there stood necessary components compromised of patience and love, two eloquently intertwined details that his grandparents had carefully transformed into a gift for their depressed grandson. Being so, Einstein had done more than a serviceable job in reawakening Vel's lust for life, and high speeds of course.

In fact, Vel had began the ill fated trend of ignoring most of his household and school responsibilities in favor of big races, back roads, and broken curfews.

With each warning of, "don't let the streetlights beat you tonight," from Grandma Thelma, there were an equal amount of Vel's lengthy pilgrimages across the Dallas and Arlington metroplexes in search of he and Einstein's next great victory. Those nights would often end in blank trips or altogether minor triumphs, traffic duels with drivers feeling lucky to be behind the wheel of a new model vehicle. Other nights were much worse than the missed homework assignments and arguments over curfew with Grandma Thelma and Grandpa Charles, consisting of tickets, towings, and even the occasional high speed chase, though he secretly relished such moments.

Vel was still blatantly selfish, and though quickly maturing, still remained largely absolved from the normal standards and responsibilities of a growing young man. His past had become a crutch that he could wield around almost at will, depending on whom he was interacting with. When his grades had began to fall behind, both literally and figuratively as a priority, a letter from the school counselor would just so happen to make its way into the hands of Grandma Thelma. The letter was addressed from none other than Jessica Hillsbury. She was growing concerned about Vel, but not simply in his increasingly poor attendance record or dismal homework regime, but more so in his neglect of such wondrous potential. He was described by her as a "peculiar yet mercurial," student, one she believed to be stubborn and intelligent enough to be a future president, and still as distant as an astronaut. Even worse was his potential, to be another dropout, or teen statistic, if things didn't soon change. By letters end she had made it very clear, that she not only wished better for Johnny Velvet, but she demanded it, and at the very least it was clear that she cared.

Jessica Hillsbury was not alone in that stressful endeavor, being aided by Fred Wallace, an enigmatic shop class teacher whom had mostly stayed to himself before engaging Vel on one sunny afternoon. That chance occurrence was only initiated after Mr. Wallace had also seen enough, of Vel's growing neglect of himself, and Einstein.

"Mr. Velvet, you know it'll only give you the exact response that you give it," he began after seeing Vel frustrated with Einstein which seems to be falling apart day by day.

"Sorry about all of the noise Mr. Wallace," replies Vel, not wanting to draw any further attention to himself.

"Well, everyone plays a fools part from a distance. What exactly seems to be the problem?" asks Mr. Wallace.

"I think the stupid gears are sticking together, it's not turning over at all," answers Vel before striking the bike in anger.

"Easy young man!" yells Mr. Wallace before continuing, "no one likes a crazy man. Try it again."

Initially Vel sighs at the teachers continued instruction, but does as he's told.

"I told you, it does what it wants," he says in frustration after Einstein again fails to start. Before responding Mr. Wallace paces around the bike, observing the way it shakes and dies down to a faint putting sound. He stops at the rear of the bike, near the muffler, then reaches down and extracts a old looking rag from inside. "Pardon my empathy Mr. Velvet, but it would be akin to my wife growing upset with me for not allowing her to sleep, after she has stuffed my nostrils with Charmin," he jokes. More embarrassed than anything, relief washes over Vel's face, followed by a simple, "preciate it."

Mr. Wallace lived alone in a neighborhood located on the outskirts of Mansfield, himself also maintaining a deep appreciation for the tranquility of such isolation, and the life of an auto mechanic. After the death of his wife nearly fifteen years ago, he became a mass collector of antique cars. His favorites, a 1932 Model A Ford, a '32 Model T, and a 1923 Dodge were aligned across the his front lawn like statues of the Holy Trinity. Most of his evenings are spent working on one of his personal projects, the latest being a '36 Bugatti Type 57SC, after of which he settles into one of 'The Big Three' up front with a glass of white wine and ox tails. He listens to he and his wife's favorite musical selections, usually Louis Armstrong or Ella Fitzgerald, before finishing up and putting the cars away for the night. In a clearly therapeutic way the cars had become almost like companions, with each night affording him a comfortable remembrance of his deceased spouse.

Johnny Velvet presented a largely relatable conundrum, however distant, for the middle aged Mr. Wallace, on one hand being a stark reflection of his younger self. Watching him waste away would be akin to watching a rare collectible wither away under the guise of youth. He knew that a young man with no real understanding of his gifts was inadvertently an even bigger threat to himself than the people and world around him. Such defiance would only lead a person down a path of eventual destruction, one that he had already experienced and reconciled on his own. Three shop classes would pass before Mr. Wallace would make his move, chiding Vel in front of the class for his lack of focus and tardiness. Of course he'd known that Vel would only rebel after feeling so embarrassed, and that would earn him a week's worth of shop class cleanup. "Make that two weeks," he adds, smiling at the thought of his masterful plan coming together. After school Vel meets Mr. Wallace at the shop class to begin his assigned detention. Several blocks of cinder are positioned just outside of the main shop and need to be taken around back to the shop shed. A note has been left on top of them explaining such.

With the afternoon heat reaching its climax it takes him a full hour to complete the arduous task, which leaves him drenching with sweat. "Need a drink?" asks Mr. Wallace as he exits from the welding lab to meet his pupil. Both of them pause for a moment afterwards, Vel's look of frustration long set it, and Mr. Wallace seeming to barely notice. The sound of Vel's sweat dripping from his sleeves to the ground is the only thing that breaks the silence, causing both of them to laugh.

"I guess if the sun doesn't mind," jokes Vel in return.

After watching him down the entire bottle of water in an instant, Mr. Wallace invites him inside.

"Here is a part of the shop you students never get to see," he says as he moves aside two large refrigerators.

He directs Vel to assist him in turning the second one on its side and reaching a latch near the bottom of a door just behind. It opens like a garage revealing a partially completed antique car.

"It looks older than my grandad," declares Vel, yet still in awe of the authentic feel of the vehicle.

Mr. Wallace wastes no time correcting his quick witted student retorting, "I'm pretty sure that your grandfather would be much more open to using the word classic instead."

"Sorry, no offense sir," offers Vel to which Mr. Wallace informs him, "none taken. It's a 1930 Model A Deluxe, the only way to offend it is by neglect."

A clear view of Einstein parked outside can be seen through a small dust covered window, causing Vel to lower his head in guilt.

"No offense," jokes Mr. Wallace after himself noticing the old Kawasaki and seeing Vel's shame growing by the second.

"None taken," he replies then begins for the shop exit.

"Same place and time tomorrow?" he asks, to which Mr. Wallace promptly answers, "I imagine there's a few more of my little secrets that I could divulge. Meet me down by the old water tower instead, my house is just nearby."

And so that began, the bond of trust and patience that would begin to form between Vel and Mr. Wallace. It was an unlikely pairing from its inception, but one that made sense for the both of them. As if he could see his wife's beautiful smile beginning to set over the distant horizon, the older man sits his wine glass down on the dashboard of his '23 Dodge and embraces the last of the evening's sunlight. He blows a kiss into the wind and winks as he says, "still as beautiful as ever."

Ch.3: Graduation/The Gift

With semester's end fast approaching, and conversely graduation, Vel would need extra help to not only walk across the big stage in May, but also staying out of more motor mischief. Naturally, being such a hotshot behind the wheel came with its own vices, a necessity for big time thrills, and that meant if he wasn't working on car projects with Mr. Wallace, all bets were off. By his grandparents account, "if the ability to cause stress were a job, he'd become the family's first millionaire, many times over!" At the recommendation of Ms. Hillsbury, the senior would receive special consideration for a full ride scholarship from UT's burgeoning mechanical and tech program, if only he could stay trouble free after having his entire juvenile record expunged. Besides, most of his trouble could be attributed to normal youth behavior such as trespassing and tagging. The scholarship would however prohibit any high risk motor incidents, as well as repeat offenders, from becoming eligible. That would mean Vel if he wasn't watched closely, and after putting her name on the line for him, Ms.

Hillsbury would prove staunchly determined to not allow that to happen.

At eighteen Vel had also began to watch closely on his own time, her that is. Though he would often pretend to be totally unaware of her presence, there was not a chance that he would actually miss her spying on him from any distance. For him her beauty was only met by her vigorous passion, all of which would eventually be needed. Vel's past had yet to be completely shaken. Remember the big rally on Prom Night two years ago? Well, after that an all-points bulletin(APB) was made by the hot tempered sheriff, Caldwell Henderson, regarding the seriousness with which reckless motorists and street racing were to be addressed. He was way past the point of incarcerating offenders, many of them still young, he wanted to see them completely brought to ruin. The message was thoroughly spread across the next several counties, and a special tactics unit was formed within Mansfield's own ranks, to be headed by a hell bent captain in Henderson.

For the year or so a stiff punishment was handed down to seemingly anyone behind a steering wheel after dark, especially if they were caught in the act. Just seven miles over the legal speed limit, in any part of town, and you were automatically considered to be a high risk motorists, and charged as such. With the parameters for driving set so strictly, Vel would barely have room to walk, let alone be caught illegally on Einstein. Sheriff Henderson was desperately on the lookout for the black kid on his green bike, performing relentless searches on school yards as well as personal garages. There weren't many black families in the area, so it would only be a matter of time before he would pay a personal visit to the big house on the hill, the one belonging to Grandma Thelma and Grandpa Charles.

The first time that his cruiser pulled up Grandma Thelma was out front in her stunningly delicate garden full of flowers, fruits, and vegetables. She too was an avid collector, of scented flora, not that the hardened Sheriff Henderson cared to notice. After being on this Earth all of seventy seven years, hardly anything bothered her old soul, even law enforcement. Stepping on one of her babies, which Sheriff Henderson had done, or messing them, was still a huge mistake. Before he can even speak Grandma Thelma addresses him about where he stands, "you know officer, God made enough room on this planet, for even uniformed men to keep their feet on firm ground." Sinister in his own right though, Sheriff Henderson catches the intent of her remark and looks down at his feet planted atop of a prim rose's stem. Without hesitation he presses down and twists his foot, snapping it in half.

"Mam, I have information that might place," he begins, as Grandpa Charles exits onto the porch. He finishes, "a resident of this address in the act of a motor felony a few months back."

Before his words have time to settle Grandma Thelma, still upset about her flowerbed, snaps back, "well if it happened so long ago, what just now brings you up here?" The sheriff's blood quickly begins to boil, but he maintains his position.

"Mam, it's called an investigation, " he snidely answers.

"Well officer, if you have anything further to investigate on my property you can deal with me," demands Grandpa Charles, his sudden approach catching the sheriff off guard.

Sheriff Henderson takes a brief second to respond, but accepts the elderly man's words, as nothing less than a challenge of authority. His lone question, "sir can I see some identification," creates a frenzied domino effect of unfortunate events for both Grandpa Charles and Vel.

Apparently Vel had kept several traffic incidents, in his grandfather's name, under the likes of his own namesake. In fact, he had kept his night life a total secret, masked behind after school evening's down at Mr. Wallace's and late night trips to the local Walmart. He never liked lying to his grandparents, so he never quite told the full truth. First there was the 60-roll on the North Dallas Tollway which was smoked out in under twenty meters. A single cruiser dare gave chase to the green machine, but was simply no match for Einstein's rebuilt engine. Despite Vel's astonishingly swift escape however, the bike's plates were captured by cruiser cam. Since the incident had taken place after Sheriff Henderson's county to county APB, the plate number was sent to Tarrant County to be added to the street racing database. His second slip up occurred in a battle of egos, on school property nonetheless, that saw him a split second away from being expelled. Save for a Hogsworth worthy save from the impeccably timed Ms. Hillsbury, who always kept a watchful eye, a ticket was about the best thing Vel had going for him on that day.

It was another bad day from Einstein who had been growing increasingly cranky with Vel's high speed displays, plus day to day duties. Rather than be the laughingstock over his bike's latest meltdown, Vel would have one of his own instead. No matter, his teasers were merciless, and just as Vel had heard enough, raising his gloved fist into striking position, the voice of Jessica Hillsbury would come screeching across the parking lot. Her voice, though delightful at times, would have no effect on the boys whose all out royal rumble had already commenced! Politics as usual followed, Vel being placed on a probationary graduation period and required twenty hours of anger management counseling. Again, it wasn't the worst that could've came about after the authorities arrived and started handing out more tickets than a carnival worker. Counseling would be with Ms. Hillsbury and could last the rest of his duration at Ben Barber if he stretched the hours out to three per week for the next seven weeks. All things considered it was a pretty favorable outcome for him, and Ms. Hillsbury had her a personal secretary for the time being.

When graduation week arrived it was a rather awkward time for both Vel and Ms. Hillsbury who each could sense their time together coming to an end. For Vel, it was the realization that for all of his troubles, which ultimately placed him directly under her tutelage, Ms. Hillsbury had given him a reason to reawaken each morning, even if only to have the staplers refilled by 7:15. For Ms. Hillsbury, she had watched him mature before her very eyes, and it was captivating, although she had kept two secrets from him that would weigh heavy on the eighteen year old.

One secret would come spilling out on the same day that he would walk across the graduation stage, amidst both of his grandparents and Mr. Wallace whom sat front row. Ms. Hillsbury joined them that day, in celebrating Vel's graduation and thus his scholarship to UT. At dinner is when she would tell him.

"I always knew that you were a special kid, with special things ahead of you," she reveals. Immediately her words are met by a blushing smile from Vel's usually stone face.

He manages to say, "aww thanks Ms. Hillsbury," but nothing more.

"You can call me Jessica now," she declares, signaling for him a rise in their relationship. Then she nearly levels him, looking him deep into his young fiery eyes and saying, "there's something that I need to tell you." His heart beats at Einstein speeds as she places one hand on his shoulder and the other gently up against his head, leaning in slowly.

Suddenly, if not fool-heartedly, Vel brazenly breaks into an epic soliloquy declaring, "okay Jessica I'll be real with you, I've like you since the first day I ever laid eyes on you. You challenge me in ways that I've never felt before, and I know that it all means something." She says his name in hopes of interrupting him, as to save himself from the ultimate embarrassment, but he continues, "and I know that we've always had our age and this school as a barrier, but now that I've made it there's nothing that can stop us now!" His romantic rant is indeed charming and passionate, but she knows that what she has to tell him still needs to be said. "Johnny Velvet, I knew you were a passionate rocket of emotions, ready yet to explode," she says, allowing him one last hope as she kisses him on the cheek. Then like a dagger to the heart she finishes, "but I have accepted a better paying job in

Florida that'll allow me to grow my portfolio enough to run for city mayor."

The words cut through Vel like a knife through warm butter, a sinking emptiness quickly settling in his stomach. Defeat was one thing for a high stakes competitor like him, knowing that a loss could quickly escalate from simple humiliation to deadly in an instant. Rejection however, was a totally different feeling, it's pain not so much as physical as emotional, but in instances just as damaging. In this instance, the immediacy of Jessica's message is emotionally severing to her young friend. An even worse emptiness fills Jessica simultaneously, as a crushed and embarrassed Vel storms off without warning. Tears begin to swell in her eyes, youthful in her own right. She has yet to experience the world on her own, away from underneath her father's shadow, however lucky and thankful she may have been. Now she has been burdened with knowing that she has hurt a young man that she has worked so desperately to help, one that she was in fact beginning to love.

That night Vel skipped his own celebration dinner, and proceeded not to come out of the room for weeks. A majority of those days were spent staring out of the window at Einstein. It was as if only he could understand how Vel had felt, being abandoned for such a long period of time in the aftermath. He sympathized with the bike, his best friend, but remained unmoved, stuck in his own torment. More time would pass before eventually thoughts of his deceased parents nearly saw him caste into an impenetrable shell of depression, until a fortuitous knock on the door one Sunday afternoon.

"I could sure use a hand down at the shop this summer from someone that knows what they're doing." It is the voice of Mr. Wallace who had decided to give him some space after hearing about his letdown.

Out of respect Vel answers, "that obviously wouldn't be me then."

Mr. Wallace only smiles at his crestfallen former student then responds, "just because you're use to automatics, doesn't mean you never learn to drive a standard."

Vel tries to fight it, the natural urge he feels to embrace the challenge, one that only Mr. Wallace could set forth.

Ingeniously Mr. Wallace follows up by asking, "besides, what's a real driver without four wheels?"

Not long after that, seconds really, Vel was up on his feet and ready to go! Mr. Wallace had provided the perfect motivation for him to rebound with a vengeance, giving a pep talk in which he was enamored with every word. Excited as he might have been, he still wasn't exactly clear on sure on what his mentor meant by drivers having four wheels, understanding that his vehicle of choice, Einstein, was a two wheeled juggernaut in its own right. He had dusted off plenty of four wheeled street racers in just his short time on the scene, even giving some opponents two car head starts to further test his mettle. None of that seemed to matter to Mr. Wallace who would invite him outside to receive a personal gift for graduation.

Parked in the middle of the road is what looks like another of Mr. Wallace's projects, and the motor sounds beautiful. He informs Vel that it is a 1970 Ford Escort RS1600 returned to him by another former pupil, then of the conditions under which the car must be earned. Vel chuckles at his mentor, and his project, doing his best to remain politely humble. Mr. Wallace understood that Vel's entire perception would need to be changed, and that only an inspiring performance, head to head, would do the trick. Thus a showdown would be scheduled for the next day at dawn, putting Vel and Einstein against Mr. Wallace, and The Gift.

The rules to the race are given as simple, that if at any point Vel maintains a ten second lead over Mr. Wallace, in a race for two miles, he will be declared the victor. For the life of him Vel can't figure out why on Earth the rules have been made to be so easy, almost offensive to a driver of his caliber.

"You know that we can just race the entire two miles right?" he offers, believing that he has been afforded an act of sympathy.

Mr. Wallace, dressed in a vintage style race suit, steps up to the door of the Escort, looking back at Vel before getting inside.

"I suppose it'll take that," he says calmly, remaining apparently unfazed by the rules of engagement.

When the sun rises above the last visible hilltop the race begins!

Vel uses the lighter weight of Einstein to jump out to an early advantage, appearing as only a green blur as he darts through the first twenty meters. Not to be outdone, the primed Escort roars through Einstein's trail of dust from only a few car lengths behind, preparing for their entrance into a tunnel passage that stretches for half mile. Seven seconds pass before Vel decides to look back, contemplating how he could achieve such a decisive victory, in only the first leg of the race. Again he thinks that the ten second stipulation was obviously too short, until Mr. Wallace and The Gift come blazing past him!

Einstein revs relentlessly, but hearing The Gift continuing to roar in an almighty display, offers Vel his first taste of humble pie. He's trailed before, but not like this. The tunnel is like night time all over again, blocking the sunlight the entire stretch, for Vel to turn on his headlights. Starkly contrasted in his approach is Mr. Wallace who propels the old Ford through the darkness like a ghost, both invisible yet omnipresent. Halfway through Vel loses him completely, and his senses soon follow. At first the roars were just in front of him, then suddenly they were everywhere! The spirit of the Escort had fully encompassed the shadows, swarming its competitor with the ferocity of a pack of lions, and Vel was the prey. When he moves to the right he's met by roars, and to the left more of the same, nearly making him catapult as he attempts to straighten out Einstein.

The fully risen sun reappears in a flash as he exits the tunnel, with Mr. Wallace at least five car lengths ahead! A finishing point has been marked off just up ahead, leaving Vel with about one thousand meters before he loses to his middle age predecessor. He had to admit to himself though, Mr. Wallace's chops behind the wheel weren't half bad, if he was able to make him look totally amateurish. He also knew that if anybody could climb out of a hole as deep as that one, it was he and Einstein as they had proven so many times before. Over the next two hundred and fifty dare devilish meters the green machine announces its return in a big way! The way Vel rides the bike, its front tire lifted fully off of the ground, is stunning, even to Mr. Wallace whose eyes grow wide as he watches the distance between them being shortened in his rearview. Like a veteran though, he aggressively positions himself with only five hundred meters to go. Just as Vel looks to close the gap for good, the grey Ford swerves in front of him!

For a second he thinks that Mr. Wallace is engaging in foul play, looking as if the maneuver had not only altered his route, but also his will to win. The teacher smiles in belief that he has indeed quelled his student's competitive fire in the moment. Vel though, who has fought off doubt his entire young life thus far, prepares one last trick as he again closes in on the Escort's back tire. Without pause he jerks Einstein to the right, leaning within inches of the ground! Mr. Wallace pumps the brakes, hoping that nothing unfortunate has become of his pupil. Before he can react, he hears the revving of Einstein's powerful motor, followed by Vel who bizarrely reappears near the front of his vehicle! Slightly projecting himself sideways had given Einstein a slight boost of momentum, all the while keeping him hidden in his competitor's blind spot. Mr. Wallace's brief hesitation gave Vel the time that he needed to recover, and the rest was history. Einstein and The Gift would finish in an epic tie that day, Einstein's unofficial last race, and the last time the wondrous super car would ever tie again.

Ch.4: Caught In Headlights

Of the few things that Vel does remember growing up as a kid, before the accident, is a nuance packed saying instilled in him by his mother. "It is only the honeymooners that get tired," she would say, in hopes of imparting a healthy respect for responsibility in her growing child, who on certain days would be internally incensed over daily chores. She knew that it wasn't the amount of chores, or even their difficulty, that bothered her young son, it was the uncanny consistency that she put forth in enforcing those duties. Perhaps it could explain his basically compulsive attention to detail early on. Without that consistency he would find a hard time focusing, or challenging himself, until running into Mr. Wallace.

Following their memorable showdown Mr. Wallace dedicates an entire week to showing and testing Vel over the parts and techniques of the car, and last but not least, its maintenance upkeep. He watches over him nervously as he test drives it for the first time, disapproving of its handle which grew heavier under the summer sun.

Mr. Wallace frantically yells, "easy, easy," barely able to continue the demonstration with Vel unable to smoothen his hard turns.

"It moves like it hasn't been driven in years," declares Vel as he exits the vehicle and hands back the keys.

Rather amused by Vel's novice response Mr. Wallace explains, "just as with life, every road becomes more difficult when our problems are exposed in the light."

Obviously agitated Vel chides, "well there's quite a few that need fixing here."

Mr. Wallace is unapologetic when he declares, "cars only reflect their drivers," an idea that Vel was apparently unprepared to embrace.

After storming off for a few hours he would return that evening shockingly refreshed, his confidence for whatever reason being completely reinvigorated. When asked of his renewed poise, replacing what had been a short fuse, Vel simply announces, "I've graduated." The stoic look in his eyes confirm his commitment, not once removing them from The Gift since returning. Ironically, it is not only Vel that experiences a total shift in perspective and thus performance. The car itself once again moves sublimely underneath the stars during Vel's nighttime testing trials. In ways indescribable the solar light being emitted from the moon and stars combine to reflect off of the car's body, making it nearly invisible!

"Whoa! Okay you have to tell me what's up with this thing!" demands an ecstatic and altogether bewildered Vel after exiting the car.

"Well, it is rare model," humbly answers Mr. Wallace, but Vel won't hear any of it.

He clarifies, "you know what I mean Mr. Wallace, it's like the car has an alter ego or something," as he circles the vehicle looking for hidden alterations.

When he rises again, it all clicks for him. He quickly re-approaches Mr. Wallace and determines, "it was how you were able to catch up with me so fast when we raced, wasn't it? It was why I couldn't see you."

Finally ready to ease Vel's steadily racing mind the older man speaks revealing, "the car's parts form an anomaly, their cosmesis being due to a certain change in the nighttime atmosphere."

"It felt as light as a feather, like I was riding on air!" declares an even more excited Vel.

Mr. Wallace begins to answer, "the current of solar power that flows through the car," but is abruptly cut off by his giddy former student who confidently proclaims, "makes it absolutely unbeatable!" Seconds later he is impatiently out of the door.

Vel would terrorize the night street racing circuit unencumbered for the next three weeks, with his car and exploits after nightfall quickly growing in fame. As a reward, and for extra intimidation, he had given The Gift a new paint of coat, more black than any paint that he had ever seen. To even the most savvy veteran's surprise, none of the competition stood a chance, with the Ford's mysterious elusiveness becoming the stuff of legend! No driver, road, or surface was safe with Vel and his menacing new machine on the streets, and that was just the way that he liked it. For all intensive purposes though, being a stalker of the night was not at all what Mr. Wallace had wanted for his former student, or The Gift. He knew that Sheriff Henderson's suffocating PBA against young motorists still stood, yet Vel had ignorantly been lured back into the lifestyle. It was no wonder that his visits to help out at the shop had gradually come to a halt. It was then however that Mr. Wallace would begin his investigation further into the matter. What he would find would leave him astounded, and greatly disappointed.

On a warm summer evening after the sun had finally disappeared, to be replaced with the starry night sky, Mr. Wallace would park his car in an empty parking lot of an old bank located on Beach Street in Ft. Worth, almost twenty miles away outside of Mansfield. Whether it be his evening zest for a tasty

Mocha Latte, his experienced intuition, or just plain luck, Mr. Wallace would stumble upon the old Ford just as he had thought. A flamingo colored EG Coupe passes through the intersection traveling at least 85 miles an hour, but doesn't raise Mr. Wallace's suspicion as he carries on sipping his latte and listening to oldies. Less than ten seconds later a silver 240SX shoots through the same intersection and onto the highway, moving fast enough that the s13 appears as a strike of lightning! It was also fast enough to raise the shop teacher's suspicion, that something "extracurricular, " may be taking place. Confirmation arrives in the form of the next vehicle that passes through the red lights awaiting at the intersection. Then he watches as his mocha begins to tremble in its cupholder, followed by the sound of a roaring engine! The roars are familiar ones, but no less startling as he snaps his head to the intersection. This time he can't make out the make or model of the vehicle that passes through, only a dark aura that seems to send shockwaves through the ground. Every piece of paper in Mr. Wallace's car goes airborne as a result, after of which he starts his own motor and begins his pursuit!

Another Honda approaches swiftly as he hurries to take the on ramp onto the freeway, nearly sending his 1965 Shelby crashing into the concrete infrastructure! He grits his teeth and holds on as the mustang just misses completely spinning out.

"Well I'll be John Brown," he says in disbelief of the reckless driver.

This was no time for him to be shaken, being quite the driver himself, he had to find Vel before trouble could. With the roars already sounding over a mile away Mr. Wallace puts the Shelby into gear and flies onto the freeway behind them.

Unfortunately for Vel, if Mr. Wallace could hear the roars of The Gift as it had closed the gap in the race and taken the lead, then so could the local authorities. The sounds of their sirens are heard shortly after, signaling that the race was indeed being smoked out. Mr. Wallace's heart begins to beat rapidly as he sees the red and blue lights swarming, understanding that if Vel was to be caught the litigation that followed would be endless, enough to potentially keep him out of school in the fall.

In a rather poetic scene of justice, Mr. Wallace passes the ill-mannered driver of the Honda just as he is being placed in the back of a state trooper's car. The other officers have relentlessly continued their pursuit of the flamingo colored coup, as well as Vel, neither of which plan on going easily. One officer's car stays neck and neck with the Coup as both of their dashboards read 110 miles per hour! Amazingly, them and two other cruisers struggle to keep pace with Vel, let alone sight of him. Like the daredevil he is, Vel abruptly steals a page from his mentor's book, and ghost rides The Gift! The officers seem shook, each of them taking to the radios in utter disbelief, feeling the thundering roars begin to encompass their vehicles fully.

"Ha, you can't catch, what you can't see," arrogantly declares Vel, just before meeting his match, sort of. Caught in the haze of his own confidence he becomes unaware, and unable to see, what lies ahead. Against protocol, and by the word of Sheriff Henderson, local troopers had dangerously laid a spike strip meant to take out the car's tires. At the speed Vel was traveling, such impact would easily leave The Gift overturned! As a grizzled veteran Mr. Wallace understood clearly how these events unfolded, as Vel would soon find out, meaning he had a mere seconds to warn him! Cunningly, he flashes his headlights repeatedly, desperately hoping Vel would notice. Looking confused in his rearview for only a moment, he hits the brakes and prepares to exit, before a resounding boom occurs!

Ch.5: Life Without Speed

Some things in life have to be experienced, more or less, before there can be a full understanding, and appreciation, of what was. Every person has them, the complex nuances that make us who we are, both good and bad. They make us therefore, a sum of our experiences. In each of us, there lies a motive to our motors. As Vel would find out in his latest brush with mischief, he too was no different, a mere mortal on a seemingly infinite plane of existence. He too was stuck with no light at the end of the figurative tunnel.

His slight moment of distraction, provided by Mr. Wallace, had prevented the aftermath of his blowout from being completely tragic. Not that his grandparents or Mr. Wallace would see the incident in any other light, their first reintroduction to Vel being his release from the jail in Mansfield. For his actions, there was a felony pending on his criminal record for attempting to flee law enforcement, reckless endangerment for driving without headlights, and of course an outstanding speeding ticket. The majority of the family's ride home from the station consisted of Grandpa Charles screaming, "Vel what the hell do you think you were doing going 137 miles an hour, in a SEVENTY!?"

It took Vel a couple of failed tries at responding to figure out that the question was a rhetorical one, and that his grandfather would only keep repeating the question the more he tried to answer, even against Grandma Thelma's warnings about his rising blood pressure. If that wasn't already bad enough, it wasn't the worst part. That would happen to be next in the sequence of unfolding events, finding out that The Gift had been removed from the freeway on a tow truck, and ordered to the scrap metal yard by the cruel Sheriff Henderson!

By the grace of some higher power, Vel wasn't religious much, the vintage vehicle was still registered under the name of Fred Wallace. Turns out the shop teacher had made it down to the scrap yard just before they were turning on the crusher! Not only had Vel gotten into the most trouble he had ever been in, incurring the wrath of even the usually silent Grandpa Charles, but in all probability he had betrayed the trust of the one man outside of his immediate family that actually cared for him most.

Mr. Wallace didn't have to seek the right to have The Gift returned, it was already his. He knew the ins and outs of the car, it's strengths and weaknesses, because he cared to know. That is what Vel would find after watching Mr. Wallace care for the gift day by day in the aftermath of his idiocy. The worst part is that time would only make the distance from which he'd been reduced to watching from, only seem further with each day that passed. Now he would have to rely on true courage, to pull himself out of such a hole. First though, he would have to find some.

That wouldn't come as easy as it sounds, for a young man that hadn't had too many examples of courageous figures in his own life. On the surface of things, there was Grandpa Charles who rarely spoke a word out of character, a model of temperance for most of Vel's life until recently. There had to be courage he thought, in the consistency his grandfather had displayed for all those years of military service. Through good and bad, he had held on and stayed with his family, though in silence, and though it was to be respected, it wasn't exactly the courage that Vel was in search of. Being silent would only caste him further into the spell of depression that was slowly overtaking him.

That only left Grandma Thelma, the voice of the Velvet family, considering the malfunction of most of the men that had come along, save for Grandpa Charles. She was the antithesis of her husband, though she had grown considerably more gentle after tragedy struck the family. Before that she was about as courageous and fiery as they come, a beautiful southern belle of her time, and an explosive madam of resiliency thereafter. She still could be an inferno of attitude in protection of her family, especially Vel. It's why she barely spoke a word of chastisement on his ride home from jail. You could tell in her face though, that she was more hurt than anything, to see the fatalistic spitting image of his father that Vel was becoming. From his point of view, his recent troubles would only allow her too see him as such, not her beloved grandson.

Unintentionally such thoughts would bring about only deeper manifestations, those that Vel had buried deep within his core just to keep up with an otherwise chaotic world around him. He recalls the feel of his mother's soft curly hair, matching his father's black leather jacket, as he looks at the only picture that remains of the couple. It's a wallet sized photo from the 90s, partially smeared and wrinkled from years of tears and squeezing. Now there were more tears, though no strength was left to squeeze.

The longer he would stare into the picture, the more he would begin to see himself, in his father. More unnerving, was every visit to the restroom where he would in turn see his father in his reflection. There was nowhere that he could run, and even fewer places to hide. Grandma Thelma kept a house full of antique mirrors, which only further insured his seclusion. During one stretch he didn't leave his room for an entire month, causing even Grandpa Charles to relent and begin to show concern. He offers to take Vel to the Mavericks basketball game, knowing that his grandson is a Dirk Nowitzki fan. "I hear the Mavs have a real sleeper in that Dennis Smith Jr. kid," he says, hoping to spark a conversation. Instead, Vel declines with a simple, "I'm good, thanks," as he continues to stare at the ceiling.

Another week passes it seems before sunlight enters his room again, this time as his grandmother snatches open the blinds for "her plant's sake." When she does, an irritated Vel gets up and storms out of the house altogether. Against the warnings of his grandparents, and despite his pending criminal status, he hops aboard Einstein once more and hits the open road, with no thought of ever turning back. "Can't believe it'd just be us two again huh?" says Vel, left talking to his old companion Einstein after about fifty miles or so. At 150 miles the conversation changes, to his emergency need for gas, and the only stations being miles away!

Though the water tasted funny in whatever little Texas town that he would push Einstein to, their hospitality was about as genuine as it gets down south. After figuring out that he had made the bone headed mistake of leaving his wallet, Vel is luckily able to catch a ride back to Ft. Worth, with a comfortable spot for Einstein strapped down in the back. From there an old friend, Kyle Roberson, would give him a lift back to his grandparents home in Mansfield. Another big surprise would be awaiting his return however.

"Are you sure this is still your pad man?" asks Kyle, chuckling as they pull up in front of the house. Everything inside of Vel wants to laugh with his friend, but he's swift to see that his friend isn't joking at all. Not that it was hard to see either, Vel's bags had been unceremoniously packed for him and placed on the front porch. Regardless of the two Oldsmobile's being parked in the same position as they had been for weeks, and the sound of thunder beginning from the heavy rain clouds above, Vel's phone calls and knocks at the door would continue to go ignored. Maybe they had finally had enough and grown tired of his stubbornness and unpredictability. Even his grandparents stress levels had to have limits, despite how much they had loved him. That left only Mr. Wallace, as someone that Vel could turn to. Sure him and Kyle had grown up together, but he was soon to be married and already skating on thin ice with his fiancé. It was either now or never, for his courage to come full circle, and afford him the strength to apologize to his mentor, his friend.

That night as the downpour of rain began Mr. Wallace sat in front of his old television set, watching old VHS tapes of he and his wife. Every now and then he'd get up and change the old jazz selections playing on repeat and refill the two wine glasses that sat on a small coffee table. When the next round of thunder seems to carry on for more than a few seconds, he rises to his feet and walks towards the window. Then he hears more thunder, which he discovers to be none other than Vel knocking at the front door.

"Well good evening young man," he says, inviting the soaked teen inside.

"Thanks Mr. Wallace," answers Vel, avoiding immediate eye contact as he enters.

After offering him a drink, to which Vel declines, the two of them have a seat on the couch where Mr. Wallace was sitting.

"It's getting pretty bad out isn't it? Shouldn't you be home?" he asks, after noticing Vel wouldn't be the first to spark up a conversation.

"Nobody's home I guess," responds Vel, just as empty as the look on his face.

Mr. Wallace of course knows what that means, and gives the young man some time to think to himself, tuning back into his homemade videos.

At least an hour passes by with still no one speaking, just old jazz tunes running in continuous rotation, and of course Mr. Wallace refilling the wine glasses for the last time. As the the next song begins, one slower than the others, he glances somberly at the television screen at a dazzling image of his wife. To his credit, Vel notices.

"You really miss her don't you?" he asks, causing Mr. Wallace to snap out of his daze and sit the two glasses on the table.

He smiles though, and answers, "that I do young man."

"And how do you continue on?" asks Vel, knowing the feeling himself, to live on with the pain of such great loss.

In his former student's face he sees such a familiar image, of himself, and pain.

He answers, "well, you learn to live with it, still coming home as if her face will still be waiting for me when I open that door."

After taking a final drink of wine he puts the cork back inside the bottle and admits, "I tell you what, putting all of the pieces of your life together becomes a hell of a lot more difficult without her."

"Hey Mr. Wallace, I'm sorry you know, about the car and everything," interjects Vel, unwanting to dive further back into his own thoughts of loss and emptiness. Besides, all Mr. Wallace seemed to have was his tapes, his wine, and his cars.

"Don't worry about that kid, you have to grab life by the wheels sometimes!" he declares, clearly the after effects of the wine setting in as he partially stumbles.

"Just know where your blind spots are...and please, stop for all law enforcement," he pleads, before stumbling down the length of the hall and into his bedroom. As Vel sat back on the couch and attempted to fall asleep to the soothing sounds of Miles Davis, he would think to himself, there's no better gift than a friend.

Ch.6: True Professionals

Mr. Wallace had always told him, "stay ready, so you don't have to get ready," at nauseam, as a way of teaching him the rewards when rigorous preparation meets chance opportunity. That meant being ready for everything, both positive and negative, because the cherubs of resiliency produced by hard work could sometimes override bad circumstances. With Vel in his current predicament, under a cloud of such ominous forecast, those lessons would have to surface sooner than later.

Based on Vel's building criminal background, and the evidence against him in his pending cases, word would reach Mr. Wallace via email, that Vel's eligible status had indeed been revoked until the following year. Upon receiving the news, Vel was in pieces, and Mr. Wallace had to do something to get his pupil out of the miserable rut he was in. With little work left to be done around the shop, he offers to him the opportunity to put his driving skills to the ultimate test, in the form of the National Semi-Pro Racing Circuit. He had put in a few phone calls and gotten Vel an official testing trial in August, leaving him absolutely ecstatic! The NSPRC though was for only "the best of the best amateur racers from across the nation," as Mr. Wallace explained before warning the excited teen, "so you better put on your big boy pants."

Of course he would be driving The Gift in competition, but Mr. Wallace wouldn't make it so simple getting it back. He would have to earn it. Again using his connections, Mr. Wallace would arrange a couple of pre-trial exhibitions at a track in Dallas, to test his Vel's mettle. In the first race of the evening, against another former student of Mr. Wallace, Vel would be faced off against a Nissan Skyline GTR. The turbocharged R32 would get off to a ridiculous start, churning around the track relentlessly with Vel trailing behind the entire first lap. Remarkably, as the first stars begin to appear in the sky, The Gift unleashes a mighty burst of speed! Vel winks at his competitor, as well as his mentor, before taking the lead for good.

The second race would take place under a full moon, and would test not so much Vel's speed, but his character. His challenger, driver of a new canary yellow Porsche 911, had been regional champion two years running, and four of the last five! With such a prestigious reputation at stake, this favor was harder for Mr. Wallace to come by, and thus would be kept between the three of them. Being that he was moving up to the pros soon anyhow, it still wouldn't stop the precocious young champion from pompously proclaiming, "there's absolutely no way that thing is going to beat me," after seeing Vel arrive in The Gift. His arrogance would leave Vel fuming, but they would wait a little while longer for Mr. Wallace to show. When he finally did, the two drivers were already at the starting line with there engines revving with attitude! Mr. Wallace is pleasantly surprised to see the two already so acquainted, even if it amounted to bitter disdain for each other. He allows both of them to see him clearly before signaling the start of the race, steadying them for what will certainly be a highly competitive five lap match up. When he signals for them to go, both cars furiously bolt down the track!

The first lap sees the Porsche move phenomenally around the track, as Vel does his best just to keep up. Even when he does come close to the Porsche's taillights he's quickly cut off and pushed back, unable to maneuver around his foe. The next two laps would be much of the same, except now Vel was growing desperate, and fast. Halfway through the third lap he sees a small opening coming up as they prepare for a turn. When he takes it, the Porsche swerves into the space, tapping it's brake lights! The maneuver almost sends The Gift spiraling into the wall! Now Vel is certain, his competitor would stop at nothing to protect his pristine reputation.

Maybe that sense of rogue energy was exactly what he needed, or the arrival of the moon in it's fullness, but either way he would suddenly start driving as if his life depended on it. In a sense it did if he didn't desire a life working late night shifts in somebody's warehouse. During the fourth lap, Vel would look to take control of the race, by forcing his opponent to become the reactor. Of course his adversary could maintain a lead if Vel allowed him to comfortably do so, but that wasn't Vel's style at all.

The next opportunity that he saw, a quarter of the way through the fourth lap, he took it! This time instead of shying away and allowing the Porsche to dictate the pace and space between them, Vel does the opposite, charging the much more sturdily built Ford directly forward! The Porsche's driver would indeed react in complete disgust, seeing The Gift's steel bumper pressing up against his rear fender. The slight contact would nearly cause the Porsche to spin out, forcing it's driver to brake momentarily. Vel's aggression would afford him with just enough space to inch into the lead, where things really got interesting.

Once again the mysterious Ford would haunt it's opponent, roaring loudly as it's engine seemingly grew unequivocally stronger! The Porsche's driver is absolutely stunned, and the ability of the old model car to keep pace at such speeds. As the two racers begin the fifth lap, a oily solution appears to have leaked onto the track just beyond the halfway point, too early for either of them to have noticed! Vel, in first place, is the also the first to see the slick solution awaiting dangerously in the middle of the track. He looks back in his rearview, and into the eyes of his competitor, maniacally crave victory, regardless of the dangers. No matter, victory would surely be Vel's if he were to just floor it in a straight line to the finish, knowing for certain that the Porsche would be pressed to max speed out of sheer desperation. If the driver were to maneuver wrongly though, while traveling at such speeds, his car would instantly be flipped and broken into pieces!

Only a monster could allow something like that to happen with full control to prevent it. Vel was ferocious in competition sure, but he wasn't truly a monster. Besides, he understood that it was his own arrogance that had been his life's undoing, and he couldn't stomach someone else's on his watch. With only little ways to go Vel downshifts and takes the inside lane, gliding directly across the oil! The Porsche driver simply laughs, seeing the move as none other than a rookie mistake, before maxing out his vehicle and cruising to victory.

"Guess that's a DNF for you bud," he says promptly after exiting his vehicle.

"DNF?" repeats Vel, confused by the insult, or perhaps his lack of reasoning.

"Did not finish!" he declares loudly, seeing the steam building within Vel. Before Vel can snap back he reminds him, "get more than three of those during the season, and you automatically fail to qualify for regionals"

After hearing his warning Vel doesn't reply, allowing Mr. Wallace to come embrace the both of them after their heated contest.

"My, my, what a mighty display the two of you put on!" he declares with the fervor of his youth.

"You mean I put on," retorts the Porsche driver, oblivious to the nuances of his own victory.

Mr. Wallace smiles at Vel's frowning face before congratulating the winner at once.

"Yes, you emerged victorious, as you should expect," he starts, letting the victor briefly bask in his accomplishment before continuing, "but both of you proved to carry the qualities of distinguished champions to be!" Not being exactly what he had wanted to hear, the young driver would enter his Porsche and zoom away, leaving Mr. Wallace and Vel to their ways.

"You knew didn't you?" asks Vel immediately after his opponent's departure.

Mr. Wallace calmly maintains, "I haven't the slightest idea what you're talking about."

"You knew about the oil on the track Mr. Wallace, I know you did!" declares Vel, challenging his mentors answer with certainty. Before the teacher can respond

Vel adds, "just tell me why you didn't want me to win."

"What I can tell you," says Mr. Wallace pausing for a moment, as a proud father would, before continuing, "what I can tell you, is that I've always known you to be a big hearted kid, and that won't change."

After getting The Gift registered under NSPRC guidelines, which included the exclusion of Vel's favored leather jacket, he would finally be ready for the opening race of the season. Stipulations would require him to finish in the top seven to qualify for the remaining contests of the season. He would be afforded three opportunities to succeed, or else be rejected by the circuit. It was considered an easy goal to Vel, who would be warned by Mr. Wallace to not let the same overconfidence befall him once more. All it would take was one bad start at this level, and Vel would be packaged with The Gift, one way express back to Mansfield.

"Circuit racers ready! Go!" screams a flag bearing man in all black, signaling the start of Vel's first official semipro race! Immediately he can tell the difference in the traction of The Gift's tires on track, which given the scolding Texas sun seems about as equivalent as riding on tar. The car's frame drags along heavily around the first major leg of the race, leaving Vel well behind pace in 22nd place, and rapidly searching for answers. "Think, think, think," he says to himself, believing that the vehicle's gears may have began to stick. Two cars are positioned a few lengths behind him to the left and right, with another two just ahead. Ready to make a move into the opening between the two up front, Vel counts to three before striking. When three arrives, the cars ahead of him both push inward, pushing Vel back into a tie for 25th place as the other cars from behind join them up front! It is the unfolding of a dreaded last place finish.

"Team racing!? When were you gonna tell me about the buddy brigade you were signing me up for!? At least I would've known what I was getting myself in to!" yells Vel, steaming with frustration over his first race on the semipro circuit.

Mr. Wallace sees that the stiff competition has taken its toll him and replies, "It's not the worst that could happen Vel, there's still at least two more races for you to do it. Those are sponsorship teams, that's all."

"And who's looking to sponsor a little black kid with a felony on his name!?" retorts Vel, to which Mr. Wallace instantly corrects him.

"Pending felony Vel!" he declares before expounding, "if you don't stop living in the past then it'll live through you. You can take the good pieces with you, or the bad ones, but it's you that has to choose."

Although he is frustrated, Vel grits his teeth, shaking his loathing self pity, and remains undeterred. Training for the next race would be a blast for him, and another chance for the student to challenge his teacher. As exceptional as he might have been at the rudimentary principles of racing, there still were advanced techniques that if mastered, could begin to put him on the offensive. At one point in their exhibition, Vel holds a considerable lead on Mr. Wallace in his rebuilt Shelby. The two cars come around a tight bending curve, a point in which Vel naturally eases his foot off of the gas pedal, but as he soon learns to his disadvantage.

As the turn grows even more narrow, he sees Mr. Wallace execute an unbelievable maneuver, steering sharply toward the outside of the curve, lifting off of the throttle and then tapping his brakes! The mustang's weight shifts, causing it to flawlessly rotate around the turn while maintaining it's incredible momentum. At the exit of the turn Mr. Wallace charges the Shelby into the lead, leaving Vel stunned in disbelief! Though he would recover and defeat his mentor, there still stood a vast difference in experience between the two, and Vel could feel it. In fact, his blood boiled because of it.

"So how many secrets do you have exactly if you don't mind me asking?" snidely asks Vel as the two work on their cars a short time later.

"Well there's a few things only age and experience can teach you," answers Mr. Wallace, who's cleaning his dashboard for what must be the third time.

"Why didn't you tell me that you used to be a driver Mr. Wallace?" asks Vel, growing frustrated all over the more he thinks about it.

The teacher hesitates but answers, "it's not something that I speak about often as you can tell."

Lost in his swelling emotions Vel snaps back, "the only thing that I can tell is that I'll never be able to compete with the other drivers if the guy responsible for training me is holding back!"

The misunderstanding wouldn't bode well for Vel's next attempt at solidifying his position on the circuit, where he would lose in similar fashion as the opener. Unable to manage the sharp turns which favored the lighter weight cars of his competition, Vel would find himself with his second DNF of the early season, and in dire need of direction. Admitting such wouldn't be easy however, with Mr. Wallace plunged deeply into his own internal battle of course. Indeed it was true, he had withheld vital information from Vel, which really only spoke to the heavy distrust that lived within him. Over the years he had buried himself in isolation, reserving his inner most passion for only his four wheeled companions.

Then came Vel, youthful and witty, rebellious even, the teen's underlying passion making them more akin than actual blood. They had both experienced severe personal loss, both outliving loved ones of their own, but their responses had been vastly different. Opposite of the preferably left alone Mr. Wallace was Vel, who admonished the need for over conversation, but could still be lured by the thrill of the chase, or race. That one distinction is where the two had remained entirely different, one regretful, and the other vengeful. Mr. Wallace's wife had been killed in a motor accident, with him as the driver, losing control of the vehicle while showboating. It's why he would never race competitively ever again, in any form, until meeting Vel.

Ch.7: Moving Backwards

Sketches of Spain plays repeatedly in Mr. Wallace's head as he rushes over to the site of Vel's third and final attempt at qualifying for the NSPRC season. He knows that it's one that means much more than wins and losses, and he wanted to be there for Vel at all costs. That would happen to include a speeding ticket on the way, narrowly missing an added attempted evasion charge for his almost comical reluctance to stop, instead doing between three and five miles per hour for two miles! Despite the officer being irate, Mr. Wallace would escape with only a ticket and the guilt of being late.

Vel wasn't nearly as spirited on this particular day, sensing his trial run on the circuit abruptly coming to an end. Again though, where most would have easily given up, or worse not shown at all, with the odds stacked so dauntingly against them, Vel was there in the middle of the storm. It was something that his mother said he'd gotten from his father, his steely resilience. He had what she called "the lucky feathers of a phoenix," for his ability to rise from the ashes of life, time and time again. Beginning the race from the back of the pack, Vel would have one last chance to pick himself up.

In spite of a rather mediocre start, by the middle of the race he finds himself in 17th place. Only a handful of laps remain, and the simmering sun has just reached it's precipice in the late afternoon sky. That didn't weigh well with The Gift, literally, which Vel could feel being bogged down in the heat. He struggles turning the steering wheel on the next few laps around the track, coming awfully close to colliding with the wall on several occasions! As his competitors scamper to move out of his way and maintain their positions, two of the cars smash together leaving fragments of their vehicles scattered across the track. A red flag is thrown temporarily stopping the race.

While his car gets serviced Vel decides to visit the concession stands, as Starburst have always soothed his nerves. Waiting in line he feels the heat, or pressure, of being on the opposing driver's home track, in this case all of them. Of course there weren't any other African American drivers in line or on circuit, just most of his competitor's family members which apparently carried a strong distaste for his choice of candy. Vel did have his own little crowd of private supporters though, spectators wowed by the mere boldness of his attempt, even if he wasn't aware. One gentlemen would approach him as he grabbed his

Starburst and headed back to the pit area for the restart of the race.

Mr. Wallace, after all of the confusion in traffic, fights to make his way through a Where's Waldo worthy sea of people, most of them on edge from the stoppage. There's a guy who confuses him for the next person attempting in line for popcorn who mistakenly blows a fuse, a lady with three crying babies refusing to move her deluxe stroller, among others, that all give a hand in further impeding his progress. After he loses what feels like valuable time in conflict, Mr. Wallace is thrilled to learn that the race has been delayed further to repair the stadium lights in case of nightfall. He finds Vel sitting in silence inside of his vehicle, completely shaken.

"How are you going to win the race if you're screwed too tight!?" shouts Mr. Wallace, startling his pupil in a very much needed surprise.

Vel does his best to mask his excitement, grinning moderately before replying, "man am I glad to see you Mr. Wallace, I'm carrying a lot of weight right now. It feels like she's dragging a ton."

"It's only responding to the tension within the driver," answers Mr. Wallace, observing the cars cooling frame as evening approaches.

Vel hears him, but has no time to be philosophical. His rebuttal, "it's kind of hard to not be tense when I feel like I'm driving in mud sir," draws the immediate ire of his mentor.

Mr. Wallace again shoots down his excuse yelling, "you're wheels will only go where you take them now snap out of it!"

Vel's spirit withholds a deep appreciation for his mentor's words, but even more so his rekindled vigor, allowing him to comfortably receive such a direct message. The challenge was set, and it was up to him to meet it.

"But what about those turns Teach?" asks Vel, starting his vehicle before adding, "I'll never be able to carry all of this weight around those tight curves, not like these aluminum and plastic cars."

"Remember the trick that I showed you?" asks Mr. Wallace, briefly jogging Vel's memory.

When he sees the lightbulb click in Vel's head he continues, "the Scandinavian Flick, get it right, and you're home free."

"You think I can make it?" asks Vel just after hearing the announcer's final restart call and the start of each racer's engine.

A white flag has been thrown, signaling that only one lap remains, making Mr. Wallace's response as critical as ever. "Well you won't exactly have time to think out there," he begins before Vel shouts his name in angst. Hurrying, Mr. Wallace suggests, "ok, ok, don't think! If you get a chance, just look." As he finishes he points to a small opening in the giddy crowd, at a neatly dressed woman seemingly intent on staying reserved amidst an audience ready to explode at moment's notice. Jessica Hillsbury has returned!

While each delicate wave of Jessica's hand is easily enough to entice her teen crush, they aren't nearly as meaningful to the fierce competition that Vel faces. Receiving a five place boost to 12th place as a result of the crash, he oozes with confidence heading into the first of three major curves during the final lap. Each of the cars all begin braking at about the same point entering the first turn, when suddenly Vel hits the gas! The other racers scurry out of the heavy Ford's way, some laughing as Vel begins losing control. He stops it just short of spiraling out, but not before he has fallen back into 20th place and fading fast!

Mr. Wallace clinches his fist watching from the stands, knowing that Vel hadn't taken into account the force he would need to change the momentum of so much weight. Jessica grips the railing, her desperation almost unnerving her instantly. She has been informed of the conditions of the race beforehand, though she had never seen him race. When Vel looks into the stands and sees her again, his eyes become filled with stars. Not from the universe of love and romance, but from the evening sky! A great distance behind even the 19th placed driver, as the stadium lights switch on

Vel smashes his foot down on the gas. The Gift explodes into the straightaway, miraculously closing in on the pack of cars ahead entering the second curve! For the second time the entire pack seems to apply their brakes in uniform, unaware of the fast approaching Vel. A few of them are stunned to see him gaining so rapidly in their rearview, but most shrug him off thinking that he might foolishly misjudge the turn again. They would be half right as it turns out, and selling him short in the process too. Vel does in fact overshoot the turn in remembering his previous attempt, when The Gift's frame felt as if it weighed double. This time however, the sable colored Ford whips around each car on the outside, narrowly missing the wall, zigging and zagging into 10th place!

Even if he didn't exactly mean to end up where he had, lady luck had carried Vel back into the thick of things, and the mean looks of the other drivers would let him know it. Beyond that, a heavy mixture of of groans, and cheers surprisingly, amount to a roaring crowd standing witness to his exploits. Their roars would hardly rival those of The Gift as more stars fill the sky, and the partial emergence of the moon. The other drivers just behind Vel quickly brake in astonishment, while the competition up front watch with dread through their trembling mirrors! If the crazed onlookers were in search of a show then Vel and The Gift were definitely fulfilling there desires.

The charging Ford moves from 10th place to 4th within the blink of an eye, with the final curve less than one hundred yards away!

In the stands, both Jessica and Mr. Wallace cross their fingers tightly hoping the best for their young friend. At this point he seems to be all but guaranteed a top seven finish and a spot on the circuit for the remainder of the season, but now it was about witnessing a something special. Without warning the three cars in front of him all begin to form a single line in what looks like an attempt to block their relentless foe. As the curve tightens, two of the racers are forced to brake, one afraid of spinning out or wrecking, and the other one being rear ended by the driver in fourth place. Though obviously not a fan of fourth place for long, the driver in third would fight for his position the rest of the way. Both would continue into the final straightaway behind first place, and the new second place holder Vel!

He had performed a physical miracle, splitting two vehicles while executing his mentor's mud racing maneuver to perfection, shooting into the last straightaway bumper to bumper with first place! His competition fights viciously, beginning to feel the heat, of being hotly contested by such a devastating newcomer. Vel and The Gift's arrival on circuit would certainly be a threat to his position atop of the NSPRC pecking order, and they were announcing so in a mighty fashion. When he gets his lone glance at the menacing culprit through the window, appropriately Vel gives him a look befitting of a staunch rival. Vel too is stunned, to see a Ford Focus Rs Rx being driven so powerfully, so determined. It hits him as he crosses the finish line, Mr. Wallace and Jessica celebrating wildly together his first place finish, that the other driver was the unpredictable Chayne Chambers! As his two lone supporters continue on frenetically, Vel, like the onlookers around them, stares blankly in venomous silence.

Later that evening the group has dinner at Mr. Wallace's place commemorating Vel's big victory. The guest of honor however continues his introspective stoicism, leaving Jessica no choice but to interrupt. It is their first time reconnecting in person since her return.

Hitting him on the shoulder she jokes, "stop acting like a sap, you just won first place!"

Vel, still clearly in deep thought, contrives a smile to comfort his old counselor.

"Or at least act like you're happy to see me," she advises him.

He rises to his feet, scooping her into his arms, then shouts, "oh Ms. Hillsbury! It's so good to see you again!”

Seemingly dissatisfied with his sarcasm she replies uninspired asking, "really!?"

He smirks at her casually before relenting, "welcome back Jess," leaving them embracing in laughter.

"What do you know about that Rx that finished in 2nd today Mr. Wallace?" asks Vel as everyone feasts on the teacher's home cooking. Clearly Vel hasn't been able to shake whatever it is that haunts him, but Mr. Wallace jumps at the chance to discuss the details of the race.

He reveals, "the Chambers car is like circuit royalty, a real nightmare, and a terror on any surface."

"Well I can beat him, just like I did tonight," retorts Vel, finally basking in his victory.

"Trust me, it'll be a tough road ahead," warns an ominous Mr. Wallace.

Defiantly Vel responds, "and you can trust me too Teach, I'll be in the black car you see cruising in Victory lane," before finishing dinner and exiting with Jessica.

A series of dates would follow, drawing both Jessica and Vel closer than ever before, closer than their past relationship would ever allow. Staring deep into her eyes for most of the night, Vel would find himself becoming ever so enchanted by the simplest of her heavenly nuances. Her smell would dazzle him, along with her taste for simple sophistication, were only a couple of the sources behind his uncontrollable endearment. By their third scheduled date Jessica, the beautiful enchantress that she was, has her crush eating from the palm of her hand. She even responds to his daring attempt for a kiss on the second date, with a shocking peck on the cheek that nearly floors him! Vel was as bizarre as freezing summer days in Texas though, and it wouldn't be nearly as easy as it was appearing, reaching his true inner sanctum of emotions.

On the night of their third date, Jessica makes plans to surprise Vel with a place that feels like a second home to him, his favorite restaurant in the world Sweet Georgia Brown! Considering that Vel had never even ventured outside of the Texas border, the home style soul food spot in Dallas would have to due. The date wouldn't be an ordinary affair either, she had rented out the entire thing for just the two of them, with hopes of a fancy candle lit occasion. Two chefs were hired from the kitchen to prepare personally favored dishes for each of them, and Jessica would arrive an hour early to help with the decorative efforts.

Vel drags behind, thinking more of his ways to overcome a bad start to the race season. Typically drivers with too many, like three or more, really bad finishes hardly stand a chance at qualifying for the championship leg of the circuit, or second season, let alone winning it. Vel hadn't joined the NSPRC to make friends or even sponsorships, he joined to win. A deep rotting fear lies within his subconscious, that his competition laughs at more than fears a car which they think to be overweight and outdated, or worse that they laugh at him. He wasn't good enough to go to college, and he wasn't ready to face the bitterness of another defeat. The circuit committee had already made it clear, that even in victory, it was a mere blip instead of a forthcoming trend. They were reluctant to reward him the winner's trophy for his lone standout performance, based on his trial status. If only he could borrow his father's feathers in this moment.

"Madam, are you sure he received your invitation?" The chef's question breaks Jessica's long concentrated silence, frozen by Vel's absence.

"Oh yes, he's just running a little late," she says in return, more in denial than anything.

Of all of Vel's young or off putting qualities, tardiness wasn't one of them, at least not with her. If anything he had looked head over hills with a single touch from Jessica, but as the chef checks on the food finishing up in the back, she leaves a check and disappears in embarrassment.

Quickly her feeling of humiliation fades, to be replaced by fury, in her search for Vel. Now she wanted to strangle him for leaving her high and dry. In her eyes, their trust was just now being broken. Also in her sight was a flash of red and blue lights, moving at high speed down the service road of I-20! Minutes later she sees another cruiser headed in the same direction, and going twice as fast as the first! A bad feeling encompasses the pit of her stomach, growing heavier by the second, knowing that she must turn around, if only to check for Vel. Then she hears the roars, familiar ones, booming across the Dallas night! As she speeds in the direction of the roars, she sees the damning evidence. Soon after, there's an eery silence as everyone seems to have vanished into thin air, leaving Jessica with the images of The Gift's tire tracks stuck in her severely puzzled mind.

Ch.8: Love, Sweat, and Gears

The next afternoon Vel makes an appearance at Mr. Wallace's, to talk over adjustments for the next race The Turbine Seven. When he opens the door Vel is instantly caught off guard. "Didn't think we'd be seeing you anytime soon," adds Mr. Wallace, caught in the middle of an awkwardly icy stare down between Vel and a teary eyed Jessica. Hastily Jessica gathers her things and heads for the exit adding, "some people won't be satisfied until the only place left to actually show up is their own funeral," then slamming the door in Vel's face. "Man what's bugging her!?" asks Vel, trying his best to not appear snake bitten by her venom.

"Well, some of the things that we all want, may only end up in tears," replies Mr. Wallace as he moves into the kitchen.

"Who wants to sit around crying about it though?" retorts Vel following behind him.

After he pours his cup of coffee Mr. Wallace answers, "now you can't walk around being so insensitive, it's unfair, we've all lived vastly different lives."

"Oh please, she was given everything Mr. Wallace, you can just tell!" counters Vel, appearing to reject the thoughts of empathy.

Giving Vel a moment to digest his own ignorance Mr. Wallace finishes stirring the cream and sugar in his coffee then responds solemnly, "what I can tell, is that just one victory, and a lucky lady later, a certain young man is starting to fear his own potential."

"What do you mean by that!? I'm not afraid!" declares Vel rising to his feet in frustration.

"Doubt!" sternly retorts Mr. Wallace sitting the coffee down before it spills. Afterwards he continues, "every time you begin to see, even an piece of your own shadow, you run! It's called doubt Mr. Velvet! Doubt!"

For a moment there is silence, then Vel leaves without speaking another word.

On the day of the Turbine Seven, Vel is left a message from Mr. Wallace, notifying him of a moved up starting time of eleven o'clock. Unfortunately it wouldn't get around to checking his voicemail until ten that morning! He rushes frantically gathering his things and then stumbling out of the door of the Motel 6. Out of breath he searches for his car in the parking lot, forgetting where he parked the night before, but to no avail. The Gift is gone! He runs back into the Motel and demands to see the security cameras, claiming that his vehicle has obviously been stolen or towed. The clerk on duty allows him to make a full fool of himself, and then informs him that Mr. Wallace had taken the car down to the track for early race day preparations, and that Einstein awaited fully gassed out back.

The Turbine Seven was a seven surface course designed to test the circuit driver's ability on diverse terrain. It was the only track meant to simulate Alpha & Omega, or the NSPRC Championship. Vel had already put Einstein through the rigors of off road competition, the Kawasaki serving him well in his early days of street racing, but The Gift had yet to be put through such tests. Being able to drag a weighted vehicle like that around any track, let alone a multi-surfaced one, took great skill in itself. This would be much more difficult, something Mr. Wallace had already figured.

When Vel finally arrives, his guilt turns into angst when he finds that Mr. Wallace, in fact hasn't been working on the Ford at all. Even more troubling, the car is not there at all!

"Wait what's going on Mr. Wallace!? Where's my car!?" asks Vel in a panic.

"Listen, calm down," Mr. Wallace pleads, but without much luck.

Vel tries his best at reasoning explaining further, "no Mr. Wallace you don't understand, I'm sorry for the way that I've been acting, I really am," allowing a stranger to sneak amongst their conversation without notice.

Vel carries on, "I was even planning on apologizing to Jessica, I mean Ms. Hillsbury! You don't have to take the car Mr. Wallace, I know what I need to do. Besides, how will I take her out without my wheels?"

At the conclusion of his rant Mr. Wallace's silence causes Vel to turn around, where he finds Jessica standing behind him.

"Well if you would calm down for a second, you could hear me explain the plan of attack for this race. I'm not taking the car," replies Mr. Wallace after finally growing tired of Vel's frozen expression. Still in awe Vel simply answers, "oh," flashing a smile of guilt at both of his supporters. Mr. Wallace informs Vel that he believes the use of Einstein instead of The Gift would be of more benefit to him, considering the course, thus being the actual reason the Escort had been left behind parked at his house.

Mr. Wallace suggests, "in this race Einstein should be able to outmaneuver the competition, as well as do some straight line damage."

He projects like he himself was being strapped in, submerged in the intense depth that is competition.

"That's why she must've been crazy about you huh?" asks Vel softly.

The quieted Mr. Wallace pauses, his pupil's reference, catching him off guard.

He first smiles then answers, "if I must say, she would always remind me, that it was my passion that truly kept her gears turning."

The both of them laugh, embracing a much needed sigh of relief.

"C'mon old buddy," says Vel, revving Einstein's engine before shouting, "let's give em a show!"

In the race Vel would use the green machine to expose the other driver's lack of maneuverability, circumventing or shortcutting many of the tricky off road terrains altogether. He was faster through the graveyard of slick gravel, and watched as countless competitors sank in the mile of mud portion of the race. Navigating a trail through the rocks just above Vel had found a path that would prove impossible for a full sized car to use. When the rocks come to an end he jumps back onto the main road, where he is joined by leader of the remaining four wheel challengers, Chayne Chambers in the Ford Rs Rx!

Immediately Vel thinks back to their initial introduction, and him leaving Sheriff Henderson covered in mud, to help out Chayne. Vel's thoughts of the mud that fateful night seem to be extremely vivid, until he realizes that this time it is he that has been left covered in mud! Chayne was an excellent off road driver, and as Vel had stood frozen in a daydream for only a brief second, would cunningly use the mud on his vehicle in an attempt to disable him. Though soaked, the wet chunks of dirt would do a thorough job of refocusing Vel, reminding himself that both times the two had faced off it was him that had come out on top. This was only another chance for him to prove to be a superior driver, but first he had to catch up!

Traveling at speeds that were unsafe even for Einstein, Vel found that he would have to be clinically insane to try and challenge Chayne who was willing to risk it all to defeat him. After appearing to put up a close race the rest of the contest, Vel decides to allow his rival a hard earned victory, insufferably. The loss puts him one step closer to officially being out of championship contention, and in need of a breath of fresh air. To blow off steam later that night Vel would take Einstein with him, on a trip down memory lane so to speak, as he delve back into the world of street racing.

In the world of Johnny Velvet, his time spent driving The Gift, and organized racing, had somehow put a dimmer on his true passion, the freedom of the open road. Although that freedom had resulted on him losing his on a few occasions, there was a comfort under the veil of high speeds outside of track life, breaking the rules included. Even Vel had to admit though, his enhanced skills forged by organized competition. Nothing the opposition did would matter as the reunited duo of Vel and Einstein would smite all comers with startling ease. All but one that is, would fall victim to the green machine that night, Jessica Hillsbury.

Jessica hadn't stuck around for the end of the Turbine Seven, and Vel's second place finish, instead leaving to position herself for a chance encounter. She had already been suspicious of him, and knew that whatever was bothering him sat simmering near the surface, especially after a defeat. It just so happens to be a good premonition on her behalf, as she catches him in the middle of a post victory celebration, surrounded by cars in a Target parking lot. Jessica even attempts to call, watching from a distance as he dismisses the phone, in favor of showboating. This time she wouldn't leave, or allow him to escape. This time she would confront him directly.

As the crowd of cars and spectators begin to disappear in a giant cloud of smoke, Vel proudly continues his hot dog display. Lost in his own sauce he becomes totally unaware that the only person remaining there to witness his arrogance, is Jessica.

"Maybe if you had some of that out there with you down at the track, then you probably wouldn't have lost the lead last minute," she says, instantly stinging Vel who shuts off the bike in anger.

Abruptly rejecting her premise Vel replies, "forget it, organized racing is for pampered kids driving on their parents dollar."

"How would you know!?" shouts Jessica, albeit drawing a look of ire from Vel. Changing her tone slightly she asks, "so what, are you just going to run from all of your problems?"

Vel looks at her for a moment, partially upset, and entirely hesitant.

Then he deflects snapping, "and what about you, fading in and out of peoples lives anytime that you feel. You're twenty six, beautiful, brilliant, and alone! Something doesn't add up, what are you so afraid of!?"

He notices that his words, although true, may sound a bit harsh, and her watery eyes concur.

"What's got you running Jess?" he asks, noticeably more gently than before.

After crying into his arms Jessica confesses, "I'm not exactly what you think." When Vel inquires further she simply says, "let me show you."

Like Vel, her frustrations and release had secretly come in the form of a high speed companion, hers being a perfectly silver 2018 Camaro ZL1. Both her and the car were stunning, carrying a solid black stripe down it's center, and stunningly powerful, something

Vel would have to find out first hand. Jessica challenges him to a high stakes race on a piece of land owned by her father. Of course those stakes would include her request for Vel's unfathomable exit from street racing, if he and Einstein were to be defeated. Rejecting Vel's attempted offer of a two car headstart, Jessica enters the Camaro without once looking back.

The road, leading from the gates of the Hillsbury private estate to their home, stretched for nearly two miles, the first half of which Vel shows her his impeccable riding skills! Einstein throttles mightily as it devours the road underneath, going eighty five miles per hour with one tire completely airborne, then accelerating to a blazing 120 mph in the blink of an eye! Undeterred however, by his antics and awe-inspiring speed, Jessica begins to shift her own ride into gear. The Camaro catches up with Vel and Einstein with three quarters of a mile remaining, where Jessica proceeds to wreaks havoc, giving Vel a taste of his own medicine. Just as Vel clutches for his final push to the finish, Jessica turns off her headlights! The effect is damning, with Vel feeling the intimidation this time, of being swarmed by such force. This time it wasn't the mysterious aura of The Gift on full display in the night, it was Jessica. It was totally ironic, Vel being back on Einstein, and being passed by Jessica in her ZL1. Her victory would come by the same two car length that Vel had offered before the race began, to her much deserved satisfaction.

"Where did you learn how to do that?" asks Vel in the immediate aftermath of his defeat.

"It's more like I just know the road leading to our house like the back of my hand," admits Jessica, blushing to maintain her innocence.

"That was dangerous," declares Vel bringing her smile to a halt, before continuing, "but it was pure genius."

Her face lights up once again, endearing to the fact that he approves, as she squeezes him tightly. Then her cell phone rings, which she turns away to answer. Her smile instantly ceases, catching the attention of Vel who moves closer.

"What is it," he asks, her silence carrying on despite his question. "Is everything ok!?" yells Vel, growing more worried by her disposition.

"It's Mr. Wallace," she begins before turning away and letting the first tear to trickle down her face, then revealing painfully, "he's dead."

Ch.9: A Killer Coup

When morning arrives the news of Mr. Wallace's untimely death has spread across the whole of Mansfield, casting a somber shadow stretching the length of the 287. After Mr. Wallace, Johnny Velvet is the first thing on Jessica's still racing mind. She hops in her Camaro and shoots across town, first checking his last Motel 6 residence, and then the home of Grandma Thelma and Grandpa Charles. Much to her surprise he has not chosen to return home, for awhile now. His rebellion had driven him into a maddening craze for independence, but without Mr. Wallace's guidance, Vel's rage could engulf his entire world.

Jessica's next location to check would have to await until later that even, where she hoped that he'd soon emerge under the cover of night. As the sun began to fall in the sky she would await the roars, being left with only the emergence of the evening's first stars. She enters into an old coffee shop the next morning drained and fully out of answers, as to where Vel has disappeared to. Rarely has she ever sought the aid of her father and his many connections, even when it came to her prestigious schooling background, but this was personal beyond measure. Picking up her cell phone to place the call, a waitress brings her the morning paper and a cup of coffee. Before she can press dial, she sees the shocking allegations, that Mr. Wallace may have been murdered!

Originally ruled an automotive accident that resulted in the shop teacher's passing, the case was now being further investigated for potential foul play. Without making another move Jessica gets up and bolts for the door! She speeds the entire ten miles to Mr. Wallace's place which has been accordingly blocked off as a crime scene. It hasn't taken long at all though, for his treasured car collection to be removed from the property. Only their imprints remain in the grass, where his beloved, "Holy Trinity," used to be aligned. Jessica searches the premises to the best of her ability, resigning to a spot under a large hilltop tree close by. For the remainder of the afternoon she waits, nodding off to recollections of Mr. Wallace and Johnny Velvet.

Then, as a sign that unfolds underneath the heavens, a giant rumbling can be heard approaching from a mile or so away, just as the moon enters the sky. Before she can scramble to her feet completely, a massive cloud of dust begins to form as the winds have picked up tremendously! Through the cloud Jessica sees the arrival of a giant 2017 Ford Raptor, flanked by two other cars which are unidentifiable. After they exit their vehicles, three boys enter inside of Mr. Wallace's garage. Jessica accordingly moves in closer to get a better view.

On the side of the blue Raptor truck is the name 'Shark Tooth,' and all three of the cars carry a license plate reading TSA-1RCG. When she finishes taking down the plates, the three boys exit from inside. Their laughter is suspiciously insidious, their vile language containing considerable disdain for the deceased Mr. Wallace.

"Even if we didn't find the car, it was still worth it," says one of the boys to which another agrees, "yeah man there's no way that old Ford will catch this Raptor. Besides he probably won't even show, now that his buddy's a goner."

Despite encouragement from the other two, the driver of the Raptor maintains his rather serious disposition.

"Yeah let's get this over to the station, before sheriff has a fit," he says before climbing inside.

"Yeah and takes back that monster," jokes his friend as they all laugh and zoom away from the property.

Jessica sits in devastation, a witness to the entire conversation of the boys. Just as she thinks that the coast is clear, the Raptor's brake lights reflect off of her Camaro which they had somehow ignored the entire time. Furiously the giant truck pushes through the tall grass, blazing it's own trail directly in Jessica's direction! When the driver exits the car, she is hidden behind a stockpile of old tools and barrels of gasoline as he looks suspiciously at the area, eventually looking at the oddly placed Camaro. After investigating the car, and looking around a bit more for it's driver, he settles for an old gas tank sitting near the shed. He douses the entire car with gasoline, and then sets it ablaze! As he rejoins his friends on the hill, the car begins to explode, his baleful pupils fixed in the rearview mirror.

Now it was impossible for Jessica to inform her father of what was truly happening, without him sending in the entire National Guard. Going to the police station, she would find that her car exploding, even under such shady circumstances, was hardly enough for authorities to sufficiently further along or strengthen their slow moving investigation. They weren't exactly inspired to anyhow, with Sheriff Henderson at the helm. Along with a intimidating round of icy glares aimed in her direction, Jessica would see her officially filed complaint purposely thrown at the bottom of a largely unorganized pile. Before she begins to argue her rights though, it hits her! The conversation amongst the boys replays through her head, leading her to simply the station clerk for his time.

Hours later she finds herself back at the crime scene, what has become of Mr. Wallace's home. She bypasses the actual house which appears to have been undisturbed during his murder. The garage door is slightly cracked, apparently left open by the boys that had visited before. On the ground positioned in the entrance is an old car bumper which she reaches down and lifts up. Instantly she drops it, seeing that it has been smeared with blood! She observes the bumper more closely, seeing the blood form two handprints. Only Vel would possibly know how much something as inconsequential as a car part would be to Mr. Wallace, but then again he wasn't anywhere to be found.

"True drivers have a passion for the open road racing through their veins, setting ablaze a fire within them that no single event or track could ever duplicate. After you left I thought about just heading west and never looking back. Then I got arrested." Vel's words replay like an old blues recording in Jessica's head as she fuels her rental car in anticipation of a long trip. When she finishes she gets inside and takes Interstate 20, where she plans to remain for the foreseeable future, as long as her gut tells her so. After driving for over fourteen hours, outside of the Texas border, Jessica is badly in need of refueling. Both her gas tank and emotions have been totally exhausted, and her belief has also began to waiver. With only enough money left to return to the Arlington, she gasses up the car and continues on for the next few exits. Seeing nothing in sight for miles at a time finally takes it's toll as she regretfully turns the car around. She allows the tears to fall freely down her face, with the sunset settling behind her.

With one hundred miles or so to go before Jessica enters back into the state of Texas, she signals her car to exit the interstate. Entering into a small diner with only a few cars parked outside, her stomach begins to validate her stop nonetheless. She parks the rental next to an old Ford Barracuda missing it's entire bumper. The car looks like it hasn't moved in forever, if it's capable of moving at all. Then again, the entire area looks about thirty or forty years behind. She gets out and enters inside, sitting alone at a corner table.

"What can I get you this evening?" asks the teenage boy working the night shift.

"Can I start with a water," answers Jessica to which he quickly acquiesces.

"What's such a pretty lady like yourself doing having dinner all alone?" he asks after she places her order of steak and mixed vegetables.

"Well," she begins. The waiter notices that her lone utterance has been cut short, but when he looks into her eyes, she has frozen completely. He follows the length of her eyes, which have spotted Vel as he exits the diner restroom! After a teary eyed Jessica screams wildly, rushing into his arms and squeezing tightly, the slightly embarrassed waiter is stunned.

He jokes, "I hope I'm not interrupting anything," before leaving them to embrace.

Ch.10: Hide and Seek

"There's no way that Mr. Wallace was taken out by some punk kid and his friends, it's hardly likely. What about the police?" Vel's question incites a prolonged look of defeat that forms on Jessica's face, unable to quell his disbelief, just as she was unable to convince the officers at the station. Despondently she reveals, "they hardly seemed interested." Instantly Vel thinks of the station, and it's head authority figure, who's never liked him much anyway. Vel, attempting to lighten the increasingly heavy mood, jokes, "yeah that crooked sheriff probably still tastes mud when he yawns," another reference to their humiliating first encounter. Jessica knows nothing of the sort, instead being reminded of the other night at Mr. Wallace's place.

Quickly she inquires, "you said the sheriff right? How do you know him?"

Unsure of her exact angle Vel replies, "yeah we've met, pretty nasty that guy."

Jessica is left equally perplexed by his answer until he clarifies further. "Hot-tempered," he says, allowing her to piece together a portrait of the man's certainly infamous reputation. She then reveals to Vel, the incidents that had taken place with the boys at Mr. Wallace's, including the loss of her car.

Vel loses it shouting, "What!? They blew up your car!? And where was I at!?"

In his outrage Vel seems to have forgotten his leave of absence after Mr. Wallace's death, but only until Jessica corrects him.

"You weren't that easy to spot in the moonlight I guess," she jokes, reminding him of his abrupt disappearance.

Upon returning to Arlington, Vel learns that there had been validity to what Jessica had tried her best at explaining. The death of Mr. Wallace had indeed been turned into a short lived murder investigation. On the other hand, she was also absolutely astute in the way that she had characterized the poor responses of the station officers, seemingly highly irritated at her arrival. When she calls for an update on the matter, both her and Vel are shocked to hear that the case had been closed in the same undignified fashion! Without further explanation the officer on the other end of the phone hangs up.

Despite the terrible news Vel's day was just about to get worse. A second phone call, this one to his, interrupts the duo in the midst of their brainstorming silence. It's the NSPRC Commissioner's Office, revealing a supervisory clause in his circuit contract, which prevents him from competing without what they described as a "guide."

"This is crap!" he yells, smashing his cell on Jessica's apartment floor. He continues on furiously, "just say it, you don't want the black kid in your stupid league!"

"That's not what they said or mean Vel," refutes Jessica, attempting to be rational.

"That's what it sure sounded like to me!" he yells in return.

Peacefully Jessica tries again to explain, "Vel, you were in legal trouble, they were obligated to place you under some kind of supervision. It would have been irresponsible for them not to."

Almost before she can finish her statement Vel shoots her a nasty stare expressing severe displeasure in her sentiment.

"Whose side are you on anyways!?" he shouts.

Matching his intensity in a surprising display, Jessica charges at him, passionately expressing, "the same side I've always been on, just waiting for you to seem to notice!"

After she finishes she storms toward the door, but he stops her.

"Wait," he says, grabbing her gently by the wrists. He reveals, "if you leave, I wont have anybody left to fight for."

Allowing him to turn her around, the two of them share a long kiss before she assures him, "sure you will."

That afternoon Jessica and Vel return to the home of Grandma Thelma and Grandpa Charles. The look on Grandma Thelma's face is enough for a thousand words, combined with her infinite grip as she hugs him. Grandpa Charles remains reserved, but eventually gives his smiling nod of approval. Lost in their emotional reunion Grandma Thelma confesses to missing her dear grandson a great deal. Her expression leads to sobering thoughts of the late Mr. Wallace by everyone present. Conversely, those thoughts carry Vel into his next revelation, regarding his now ineligible racing status. He explains to his grandparents who appear more calm than usual over otherwise damning news. It was much more like Grandma Thelma to work up a good sweat, yelling furiously at anyone that dared to impede her grandson's charge towards success, usually with Grandpa Charles in charge of holding her back and preventing most situations from escalating. This time though, it appeared as if they had been through enough, to protect Vel. Without affording him any further words of advice or solace, they soon leave him and his guest in the front room alone.

"What's their problem?" whispers Vel, hours later after moving upstairs with Jessica to his old room. He's sure to keep his voice to a minimum, being required to still keep his bedroom door open with female guests, a rule enforced courtesy of his late father.

"They have been through a lot," replies Jessica still maintaining her position of reason.

She continues, "maybe the death of Mr. Wallace really hit home with them," as to point out their relative ages, just before Grandpa Charles sticks his head through the door.

"Johnny your grandmother wants to see you downstairs," he says.

Vel looks at Jessica, moving hesitantly towards the door.

His slow pace causes his grandfather to shout, "move ya butt boy, you act like I said you was gettin' a whooping!"

Jessica savors the moment, to see them together again, chuckling in amusement.

"What, she didn't know you still got em!?" chides Grandpa Charles before leading Vel out of the room.

As they reach the living room, his Grandma Thelma has just reentered the house with a pair of small boxes in her possession. Both of the are pretty beat up, something Vel notices immediately.

"Geesh Grandma did you dig those straight out of the garden!?" he jokes as she sits them on the table.

"Still perfect after all of these years," she declares to herself after opening one of the boxes. She withdraws a one of a kind black velvet racing jacket revealing, "it belonged to your father."

"My pops could drive!?" asks a suddenly enthused Vel.

"Could he!? He was the best I ever saw behind the wheel!" declares Grandpa Charles.

When Vel tries it on, it's a perfect fit, empowering him as he stretches his arms towards the ceiling.

A smiling Grandma Thelma then divulges, "as soon as we got the letter from the commissioner's office, we made the decision," leaving her grandson speechless.

He looks back at his Grandpa Charles who clarifies, "if you the only way they can keep you from racing is in death, then we figured it'd be the only way to give you your wheels back."

As he finishes he peels back the collar of his shirt, revealing a custom 'Team Velvet' jumpsuit, designed by his fashionable Grandma Thelma.

In his excitement Vel begins, "does this mean--," but is interrupted by his grandmother who confirms, "Charles is going to be your new crew chief."

"But how are we going to get them to ever allow it?" asks Vel, still unsure about what he's hearing.

"Don't worry, it's been taken care of," proclaims Jessica who appears from the hallway. Covertly apart of the plan all along she points out, "of course it helps to have a father in high places."

"But nobody even knows where the car is," proclaims Vel, sounding a bit pessimistic after thinking of what he was currently driving.

"That's not true at all," replies Jessica before Grandpa Charles leads the group around to the garage where they all have secretly prepared the ultimate surprise.

"So you knew about this the entire time?" asks Vel, looking at Jessica in humorous disbelief just before the revealing. Her response is rather short.

She explains, "we knew we had to get the car before it went missing too," and then allows his grandparents to take center stage.

Abruptly, Grandma Thelma admits aloud, "we knew that we were only driving ourselves up a wall, attempting to get a tiger to change it's stripes."

"So instead we thought that another change was needed," adds Grandpa Charles.

After they both smile at their exuberant grandson they proceed to open the garage.

Ch.11: Playing Dirty

Only five races remain in the NSPRC's season, leaving Vel in 8th place with The Gauntlet just around the corner. The top seven drivers of the season advance to the tri-race purgatory that will determine the circuit champion. Each of the final three races count double in the standings, and therefore stand to at least double in difficulty. Around this time of race season, with basically the playoffs approaching, the competitions turns from a singular foray into the depths of the human will, into something much more contriving, or just plain sinister.

The next race, called Grimefest, looks affably more suitable for dirt bikes than their four wheel counterparts, consisting of long peaking dirt roads, and even ghastly stretches of trudge that was suitable for no one. One false turn could land a driver in a heap of trouble, or worse, quick sand! Of course Vel had Einstein though, the easily maneuverable green machine that he had grown greatly accustomed with, in the handling of such muck. With Einstein he could be a threat to not only to be greatly competitive, but to win the entire thing, and with his fierce resolve back intact fully he was more than capable.

His greatest problem however, wouldn't reside simply in his readiness for the forthcoming challenge in the form of Grimefest, but in those who desired to curtail his chances at making The Gauntlet altogether. On race day, Vel shows up with Einstein in perfect shape, it's illuminating green color casting a magnificent emerald shadow! Most of his competition is abruptly startled, having to be reminded of their task at hand. Grandpa Charles awaits in the designated pit area while Jessica takes her appropriate position amongst the standing spectators. In her casual attire, she notices that everyone else has dressed in what looks like the most rugged clothes possible. One man dressed in full body camouflage sees Jessica and warns her, "when those kids come cutting 'round that there corner, this place is gonna be like a hog's pen." Even Vel has chosen not to debut his new outfit, a foreshadowing of the mess to come.

Despite the signs Jessica is there to stay, withdrawing her Jimmy Choo sunglasses and placing them over her face. She also takes out the Grimefest pass and pamphlet that she was given upon entrance. Before she can open it, a sudden gust of wind blows the pamphlet out of her grasp! It blows around wildly forcing Jessica to move around amusingly awkward in trying to retrieve it without disturbing the other onlookers, who all happen to be watching her in amusement. When the pamphlet finally sticks up against a restriction fence a ways from where she was seated, Jessica is lucky to be in the perfect position to snatch it. Unknowingly, she is also in position to witness Vel's very undoing. Bending down to retrieve the tricky leaflet Jessica finds herself hovering directly over the pit area of none other than Shark Tooth! It was the identical truck from the night her own car was blown to bits. It's driver, the same boy from that night as well, dons a new looking race jacket with the name Chambers written fancily across the back. To her surprise once again, the boy climbs out of the truck only once his entire time there, for the dubious arrival of the Sheriff Henderson himself!

The meeting, between the shady sheriff and the boy, is a brief one, marked by a simple exchange of an envelope and a handshake. Whatever it is that Sheriff Henderson gives the boy appears to be of some dire urgency, as he bolts from the truck disappearing into a crowd of people. Jessica's first thought is to head for the pit area of Vel and Grandpa Charles, but she hesitates, thinking of the effect such peculiar news might have on Vel during the race. As she makes her way back to her seat, opting to wait until after the race to deliver the news to him, the name Johnny Velvet blares across the intercom system. In a demoralizing turn of events she learns that his name has been scratched from the competition!

She finds him in complete silence, as if he was on the brink of imploding yet again, and this time understandably so. According to official circuit guidelines, a change in team representatives had to take place a full two weeks in advance of a driver's next scheduled race. In this case, regardless of Vel's special circumstances, considering the death of Mr. Wallace, he would be astutely penalized to the full letter of the law. Eventually Vel's stone cold silence turns into icy, slow falling, tears, with his only comfort Jessica and Grandpa Charles, standing idly by. Both of them realize that his pain is something that words have no answer for in the moment.

Arriving back at the house so prematurely seems like a funeral, with each of the humbled attendees, Jessica, Grandpa Charles, and lastly Vel, each walking past Grandma as slow paced as possible. She studies each of them closely, unable to grasp any clue of their inexplicably somber demeanors.

"Well where's your trophy?" she asks jokingly, sensibly attempting to lighten everyone's mood.

Only there was no race, not for Vel who reveals, "they wouldn't even let me start my engine."

Opposite of her usual inflammatory response, Grandma Thelma is instantly cast into a state of devastation like the rest of the group.

"So what happens next?" she asks, unsure of the circuit procedures regarding the matter.

In a defiant outburst Grandpa Charles declares, "we get ready for the next race!"

The longer he looks at Vel, remaining despondent in the corner, the more he realizes, that their brief run may have already come to an end.

Hours later Jessica finds Vel sitting under the moonlight, inside of his enigmatic Ford Escort. From a distance the entire car is invisible, until she gets closer that is, and sees him. A sullen Vel is sunken deep into the front seat when she gets inside, holding back tears of course.

"How's it going?" she asks to which Vel responds bluntly, "it's going."

Not allowing him to remain in his shell Jessica remains gently persistent.

She proceeds asking, "so, do you know what you're going to do?"

Sounding defeated already Vel replies, "I guess I'm going to keep racing, that's what everyone wants me to do anyways."

Again Jessica asks, "but what do you want to do Vel?"

This time he looks up at her, finding her eyes directly, coming to the realization that she wasn't going to allow him to remain in his self-pity.

He begins to respond, "I thought I wanted this, but after today," but is abruptly choked up by his own words.

"It's ok," assures Jessica, rubbing his back to comfort him.

He collects himself and continues, "but after today I really don't know Jess. I keep trying to find my purpose in this world, then Mr. Wallace goes, and now this. I'm never gonna catch up in the standings after today."

Though Vel's words speak to a sobering reality in which he has chosen to face the music, this time instead of opting for the first freeway out of town, Jessica hasn't taken them solely as such. To her they ring as a much needed reminder, and a potential source of motivation that was needed even more.

Almost reflexively she asks, "what do you know about the Shark Tooth?" Vel's initial reaction is only a slight look of confusion, followed by a silly Land Before Time reference. It's nearly like a brotherhood code, to not speak on fellow drivers outside the field of competition, especially a driver in which he had already had a significant history with.

Jessica sneers at him when she responds, "no Vel, the kid wearing the Chambers jacket."

Her tone is dead serious, enough for Vel to relent, "ok, ok, you're talking about Chayne. He just wanted to show off his new truck. He would've been shook if I was able to take out that Raptor with old Einstein."

For a moment he seems to regain his spark, caught in the mere thought of defeating his rival. Despite their on track differences, competition has brought about a hint of respect for such primed adversary.

He proclaims, "he's a real shark, but he's cool," much to the immediate disgust of Jessica.

"No, he's the bratty punk that blew up my Camaro!" she snaps causing Vel to gulp heavily in an attempt to eat his words. Then it hits him.

"Wait what!?" he shouts, never seeing such a bold proclamation coming.

He's caught off guard by her next statement even more so.

She reveals, "that's right, and that same kid was at Grimefest driving the same truck from that night! He's probably the one that cost you your starting spot today, him and that dirty sheriff."

The accusation is damning to say the least, that foul play had been involved in his being blocked on race day, and that Sheriff Henderson could be behind it. After inquiring further about the night at Mr.

Wallace's, Vel connects the dots for himself, his final assessment being, that the Chayne Chambers and the wicked sheriff had been tied together by blood, by murder.

Ch.12: As Far As Legends Go

To seek out each path, where fables and tires turn, is to delve into the catalyst of soul, thus the motives that drive us beyond the shackles of physical limitations. There we'll enter into our alternate, and superior, state of existence, totally subconscious, empowered solely by the idea of being, existing only as an infinite plane of black thought. There can be found little truth in power, but in truth power rests it's head for an eternity. Somewhere in the balance of it all, the need for human permanence supersedes them both, in the making of a myth, or what we call history. Becoming legendary then in itself, at least on the surface, can quickly cease from being apolitical.

The Legend of Black Velvet is shaped from the most pure form of wonder, mythos inexplicable to even those few directly confronted by it's awesome power, its almighty demand for reverence, for victory. After being withheld from participating at Grimefest, Johnny Velvet would fall into a tie with ninth place, leaving only one race before the start of The Gauntlet. Many would presume it would be his last, seeing how he needed a ridiculous boost to make a qualifying jump in the standings. With such dour expectations already firmly set in place, the stars had already began to align, setting the stage for the birth of a legend.

With Vel missing from action, Chayne Chambers had punished the remaining competition, jumping to a nearly insurmountable lead in the standings. That predicament would remain no matter what place Vel aimed to finish in The Gauntlet races, if he were to make it at all. The race on the eve of the tri-race series will be the final trek for all non-qualifiers, and only the second evening start on the semipro schedule. Coincidentally, Vel chooses what is thought to be his final race on the circuit, as the dazzling debut of his renovated Ford Escort.

The spirit of The Gift, as it was formally called, is encompassed by a large shooting star that blazes brilliantly across the sky, marking Vel's arrival on the track. Even circuit officials stand in awe of the car which illuminates in the moonlight, a magnificent streak of crimson that astonishingly shoots upward! Most of the other driver's awe quells within minutes, and the complaints soon follow. After a series of tests are done to ensure that the vehicle follows circuit regulations, the Escort is accordingly penciled in, with Black Velvet as its identifying color.

Equally as menacing, as The Gift was mystifying, was the fiery arrival of Chayne Chambers riding in Shark Tooth, with an inferno of flames bursting out of the Raptor's exhaust pipes! Awestruck officials at the event scamper to move out of his way, so unnerved that they throw a caution flag before the race could even begin. For the next two and a half miles the Graveyard, as the course known for its gravel beds ripping tires to shreds, will live in infamy as it devours each of the drivers one by one! A few of the unlucky dare chose to combat the terrain with only thicker or extra protected tires, but to foolish ends.

Near the competition's end the smell of burning rubber sifts throughout the entire arena, a sign of the carnage left behind, as well as a herculean finish. That's what it would take to win a race of this magnitude, the final one before the even more difficult Gauntlet. First those destined for such challenging roads ahead, in hopes of capturing the championship, would have to survive the chaos and wreckage that had beset them now. Most of that damage would occur on the course, as many of the very best saw their vehicles falling apart, with little they could do to prevent it. The finishing blows, and perhaps the most psychological damaging, would come in the form of two of their vengefully relentless peers.

As far as legends go, and as blood feuds would have it, Johnny Velvet and Chayne Chambers were indebted to each other. Even before they were fully aware of such fateful rivalry, their fervid spirits had already been aligned by a much greater destiny.

Neither boy could figure beyond their staunch veils of rebellion, as to why they despised each other so, although it could be as glaringly obvious as their physical differences. Onlookers, caught in a middling muse of awe and terror, would beg to differ, that the two boys bitterness towards one another had indeed made for excellent theater, the highest compliment for two amateurs with the hopes of one day turning professional.

Two miles of road is left absolutely shredded courtesy of Chayne's juggernaut Raptor, which tires are reinforced with chains. Weaving around and through the ripped up infrastructure, as well as the large rocks that move like they've been shot out of a canon in his direction, Vel was full of adrenaline heading into the final stretch! This was his style, dressed in the dazzling jacket of his father, to maintain his position in unshakable fashion, and then to haunt his opponent like a ghost! He enjoyed stalking his prey, though they wished for anything but. For Chayne, there was more to be worried about than gravel roads and the other drivers far behind him. There still remained Vel, hands firmly controlling the wheel as he comes flying over the final hill!

A quarter of the stadium's lights are designated to focus solely on the half mile finish, allowing spectators to once again become witnesses, to a wonder of the racing world. Vel doesn't attempt to control the mystical machine, he has become one with it, as it accelerates at a rate that he's never seen. Even the stadium cameras begin to register nothing but a spectacular black blur, moving at bionic speeds towards the finish! Vel knows what's happening, observing the nature of the moon, before the frame of the Escort again begins to illuminate. Several thunderous roars later and Chayne Chambers and Shark Tooth finds themselves on trembling ground, being engulfed by the awesome force to forevermore be known as Black Velvet.

Ch.13: Puppet Master/Battery Back

As tragic as only karma may allow, the sum of all human history is written of course by the victors, those fortunate enough to evade the paradigm of truth, and the painful tortures of defeat. The winners in this case, don't just sit on the royal court, or inside of the king's palace, they own it. A fortress is built to protect what has been, and to prevent what will become. Some grow addicted to this glory, the benefactors of bloody triumph, while others slave endlessly to avoid such fate, fallen by the blood covered hands of the victorious. On both sides, sacrifice watches over this infinite truth.

History then, is also filled with those that would go on to become slaves just the same, only to their own vindictive forefathers. These were tortured souls, trapped within an insidious false sense of loyalty, the helpless puppet to the merciless puppeteer. This was the hapless and ill-fated role that Chayne Chambers had been unknowingly fulfilling for quite some time, albeit with a lust for victory, and thus the temporary spoils. With every victory there came gifts and adulation, but he would learn that to some, the annals of defeat are felt skin deep, courtesy of the puppeteer.

For the majority of his twenty one year old life Chayne Chambers had nearly always taken the riskier road, a blistering courage that would become a trademark of his rebellion, and a blinding hindrance. His youthful ignorance had already led him to some dicey decision making, deciding to for go exploring institutions of higher learning in favor of open road racing leagues. The decision would create a great divide within his immediate family, the majority of which refused to support his involvement in racing. Most of his races were illegal, being underage and jobless, and that wouldn't change until prom night a few years earlier.

That was the night of his formal introduction, to a slick devil hidden behind the honor of a badge, and his eventual puppet master Sheriff Henderson. No, it wasn't Chayne's first run in with law enforcement. In fact, it would be his checkered past that would make him the target that he had became. Shortly after speeding away in the rain that night, leaving Vel and Sheriff Henderson behind in the mud, Chayne would uncharacteristically let his guard down, stopping for food at a Whataburger only a few miles away. While he's sitting inside of his car enjoying his meal, the sheriff shows up with two other cars and surround him, lights flashing and sirens blaring!

Chayne is allowed to finish his burger and fries that night, but not before succumbing to the sick intimidation tactics of corrupt law enforcement. Sheriff Henderson was the head of a criminal underworld, just like the citizen he was harassing, only bigger. The racing syndicate that he had began, protected, and lorded over, wanted to legitimize their operation through what amounted to nothing more than an easily manipulated gambling ring, the NSPCR. Needing a young driver with a mean streak, and a juvenile background to match, Chayne Chambers just so happened to be their token of choice. That started a few years back, before the more twisted side of the sheriff would surface, and real trouble began.

Of course trouble and Johnny Velvet had grown largely use to each other by the time he would meet his future rival, and he was routinely the youngest driver at most competitions, the part of foil becoming his specialty. Now he, and conversely Black Velvet, would become victims of heinous tactics, ones that would cast them both into the role of hero. While winning the last race in stunning fashion, and clinching a spot in The Gauntlet, had done wonders for Vel's confidence, his victory would effectively rattle the nerves of Sheriff Henderson. He would call on Chayne to deal him directly.

Sabotage would be the chosen method, to handle the pesky threat in Vel, and his wonder car Black

Velvet. With the batteries in his back fully activated, Chayne is charged with impairing the Ford Escort only days before the start of the circuit postseason. The daunting objective would be found readily available to attempt as Vel visits Jessica's place once again, totally oblivious to what's taking place outside. Chayne first attempts to secure the bumper of the car, reaching down with chain and hook in hand. Suddenly the car appears to move backwards, colliding with Chayne's head! In a comical sense, Chayne is furious, left confused by his own perception, or lack of depth, but he stays relentless nonetheless. He snatches the chain and hook, then heads for the hood of the car. His tussle with the hood is even more of a humorous confrontation, however worthless, ending in steaming futility. Chayne settles for simply plugging the cars exhaust system, amidst threatening backfires from the car of course!

On the day of the Gauntlet's opening race, Vel notices how his vehicle is peculiarly unenthusiastic, almost as if to be avoiding the beaming sun altogether. Where Vel turns, it turns in the opposite direction, and without any further mishandling he knows that something has gone terribly wrong. "It's not listening to me at all," he says, announcing his worries to Grandpa Charles after attempting to test drive the car for the third time. With the race's start time just a couple of hours away Grandpa Charles wisely advises him to trust the car, but more importantly to trust himself. Vel did in fact trust his instincts about the situation, so much so that in the middle of the Calle de Playa, the sand dune filled course near San Antonio, he would make a daring decision against the advise of Grandpa Charles. His decision would also momentarily stun the rest of the field and thousands of people watching, all of them watching as Vel has exited his vehicle! The decision would also come with a ten second penalty that didn't include his real time stoppage, but his car's toxic performance was more important. The probability of him dropping from the top five to the back of the pack didn't deter Vel from looking like a young man gone mad standing outside of Black Velvet. He begs the vehicle for answers, but only draws the sound of a faint revving noise in response. Just when it seems that the car is close to being totally despondent, Vel remembers the words of his old mentor, hopefully still watching from the heavens. He races around the car and sticks his arm inside of the exhaust pipe, closing his eyes when he does. "Bingo!" he screams aloud, correctly guessing the issue as he withdraws a balled up shirt from the interior. Though it's just late afternoon, Black Velvet marks it's return to the race, roaring with a spirit of vengeance!

A lot of ground separates Vel and the remaining group, those that haven't spun out or received critical

DNFs courtesy of hidden sink holes. More surprising to Vel than the number of disabled vehicles in route to his desperate dash back into contention, is Chayne, who appears to be struggling to with Shark Tooth's weight. Vel comes darting around the last bend separating him and the group like a comet, ironically finishing his rally in a tie with Chayne for third. That would be the first time Vel would see them up close, the bruises to his rival's splintering ego, and those on his face.

Ultimately, Vel and Chayne would clash for the remainder of the course, charging as high as second place while dropping no lower than seventh. Despite his depleted look Chayne would fight until Shark Tooth's weight became absolutely unbearable while trying to keep speed with much shiftier opponents. The very ground beneath him, with aid from his pesky adversary Vel, would force Chayne into a seventh place tie. Vel on the other hand would position himself perfectly for a third place finish, and boost in overall points, a small victory considering his hiccups early on. In reality he had never been closer to proving everyone wrong, by winning the NSPCR Championship, and etching out his own path in life. Proving equal in magnitude, to the burden lifting promise that such a feat would present, it would be harder than anything he had ever done.

Ch.14: Missing Challenge

Only one day of rest sits between the last race and the second leg of the tri-race series, and Vel now sits in fourth place after a skillful comeback to finish third at Calle de Playa. It counts as one of only a handful of times that he's left the area he's called come for his entire life, and considering the results, it was an exhilarating time for him. He wasn't just climbing the leader board and staying competitive in a league full of more readily equipped drivers, he was slowly winning the trust back of everyone that he cared about, and that had cared about him. In an almost methodical sense what mattered most had began to reveal itself, as it always does.

The next race, Driving Derrick, wouldn't be quite as far as San Antonio, taking place in Odessa, Texas. The name of the race is the NSPCR's way of paying homage to the big oil tycoons of West Texas, many of whom sit on the board of the circuit or have relatives driving. That would leave little time to travel back home to Mansfield for Vel and Grandpa Charles, if they wanted to be properly rested for whatever torment that they were certain to be put through the following day. Wisely the grandfather and grandson duo choose to head straight to the next meet, resting at the Plaza Inn in Midland, TX. Together they'll be in search of their first win as a tandem.

The Driving Derrick, a new course added to this year's Gauntlet, is effectively the circuit's way of simulating oil on a track. Made of few straightaways, and several slick turns, the course wasn't exactly designed to decide the fastest car in the field, but instead it was made to highlight the drivers with the best control of their vehicles. Shiftiness and quickness would be to key attributes in this race as well, but one false turn or boost of acceleration and it was goodnight! The walls of the course were aligned with iron barbs meant to constrict movement, clawing and scratching anything that came too close. A bunch of local racers are also rooming at the Plaza Inn in Midland when Vel checks in. It's a good thing that Grandma Thelma had the room booked two weeks in advance, or else they might not have been safe even in the parking lot, with all the animosity pouring off of the drivers and their teams. It spoke more to her quiet confidence in her grandson, to book the room without even knowing of how the qualifying process works, and as it was, Vel was supposed to be there. With all of the games and pranks being played amongst the different race teams throughout the hotel, one driver has remained noticeably absent from the pilgrimage to Odessa.

For a race designated to be so meaningful to circuit championship implications, Vel finds the field to be surprisingly amateurish, especially since Grandpa Charles doesn't dare to remind him every thirty minutes as he stakes out the parking lot. As a true competitor Vel would hate to have the opportunity pass him up, to duel once more with Chayne who was still first in the circuit standings. Growing annoyed from his position behind a overgrowth of bushes Grandpa Charles gripes over the walkie talkie, "you would think he was blowing off the race altogether. He's either overconfident or too focused on the final, either way these mosquitoes don't give to nickels about it. They want blood!" Even as Grandpa Charles continues mumbling in aggravation Vel remains reluctant to the idea, that his only true rival had blown him and the race off entirely. "That's just not like him, I know he wouldn't do that," he utters to himself, allowing his grandfather to carry on.

The next morning the two of them travel thirty minutes to Odessa, watching as the locals give their sloppy turns at street racing, nearly crashing in route. Vel sighs heavily watching such foolishness, which only makes him think more of his missing foe.

"Still no sign of him huh?" he asks Grandpa Charles, the designated driver for most of the trip.

Concerned with his grandson's glaring lack of focus he declares, "now is not the time to be all sentimental Vel, if he shows, then he shows. If so, we'll take him to school too."

His words appear to do just the trick, drawing a sinister glare from Vel, who looks out the window at the massive fields and giant derricks approaching then announces stoically, "we're here."

It comes with good reason in hindsight, Vel's uneasiness about Chayne's absence. He finds it baffling that the points leader would chance Vel smoking the rest of such a lesser field, which he did of course. Sure, many of the cars and team sponsors were present, but there's no way that the drivers could be the same. When he takes his suspicions to his Grandpa Charles, his grandfather advises him to, "enjoy the milk for once." How could he though, with his victory feeling so slighted. With him being in second place overall after a dominating victory, a showdown would be set with Chayne in the final. That's if he decided to show.

In spite of have a noble reason to celebrate Vel doesn't speak the entire way back to Mansfield, save for the cordial responses as to keep his grandfather's suspicion at a minimum. When they arrive back at the house, he rushes through his experience with Grandma Thelma, grabs his jacket, and bolts for the door! Both grandparents are left rather confused by Vel's inability to relax.

"My goodness, what was that all about!? I don't know whether it's a celebration or an emergency," says Grandma Thelma, continuing to watch through the peep hole as Grandpa Charles watches through the blinds.

"Well you know what winning can do to a man," jokes Grandpa Charles, tickling his wife with laughter.

Still largely consumed by a feeling of what can't be described as anything other than guilt, Vel shows up to Jessica's place riding Einstein, and dead set on finding Chayne Chambers. He desperately tries to explain to her, "Jess I have to find him. There's no way he misses that race, any track in Texas, the entire world for that matter, if i'm there he shows. Something's not right about it, I can feel it!" After sitting for a moment, skeptical at risking everything, with Vel being so close to the championship, Jessica agrees to partner with him in finding Chayne. She suggests that they first start at a place that they're familiar with, Ben Barber Academy.

Almost immediately, through Jessica's sources, they discover that Chayne Chambers had been a registrant at Ben Barber until just after his seventeenth birthday, a year before his supposed graduation date. Oddly enough, he carried no sort of GED or an equivalent either, a requirement for all NSPCR drivers. They were dealing with a high school dropout, which gave Jessica another idea. Upon searching his criminal background, she finds that his last interaction had indeed been on file, with Sheriff Henderson. All of her past suspicions hit her at once as she turns her head away from a clear image of the sheriff on her web browser.

"What's wrong?" asks Vel, keenly noticing a sudden difference in her demeanor.

"Nothing, just thinking about all of this," she replies.

If only to keep the conversation going Vel reveals, "he had a bruise on the side of his face in our last race. It looked like he was trying to hide it with a pair of goggles, but I could see it clear."

Jessica is horrified by his revelation, placing the palm of her hand over her mouth in shock. Their search must continue though.

Ch.15: A Crying Chayne

From the ashes, in the words of Vel's mother, is exactly where Jessica would start, those of a few cigarettes shared by Chayne and his friends the night that he had blown up her car. The DNA on one of the buds registers as a contaminated sample, leaving only one partially smoked cigarette to draw any plausible conclusions from, about who may have known of his extracurricular activities away from the team. With their hope quickly fading Jessica's phone rings, and a name has come back!

Bud Sanders, the eighth place finisher on the circuit this year, and teammate of Chayne's, abruptly becomes the next person of interest in Vel and Jessica's search. They find him just as he's prepared his uncle's boat for a ride out on Lewisville Lake, and is apparently not in a good mood.

"What do you want Velvet?" he asks as if expecting a visit from him.

"It's Chayne," replies Vel before preparing to explain further.

Before he can Bud warns him, "what's done is done, it's best you don't go snooping where you ain't got no business."

"We can help both of you!" urges Jessica, but he remains weary of them, continuing to fiddle needlessly with rope on the boat's deck.

After a long pause in conversation Vel and Jessica begin to retreat, their hopes apparently dashed. Just before they do Vel stops and turns back around, where he attempts to plead with Bud one last time.

He yells, "so if you don't want to help yourself, can you at least try and help Chayne?"

This causes the Bud to pause, his stubbornness being replaced with worry.

Then he reveals, "if I do, he'll kill me," so trepidly that he trembles badly.

"Who will kill you Bud?" asks Vel, slowly inching closer, but trying not to startle him.

When he finally divulges who, Bud does so in a light whisper, as not to be overheard.

"The sheriff, he's a madman," he says, with the fear of none other than Sheriff Henderson deeply rooted in his eyes.

Before they leave Bud reveals the sheriff's plan to use him as the substitute driver in tomorrows championship, as well as his organized racing scheme meant for Chayne and his teammates to win in landslides to make good impressions on the pros. Once there, even larger sums of money would be at stake, and with his authority in law enforcement the sheriff had guaranteed his partners little to no trouble in turning a profit, even if that meant blackmail. It was also at the risk of ruining young lives, that he had everyone badly caught in his web. Furious, Jessica stands up and yells at Bud for protecting him, ultimately needing Vel to restrain her. Realizing that he had already spoken too much, Bud regretfully reveals the last known location of Sheriff Henderson's operation meet up, and where he's most likely to hide Chayne.

"So what do you think is going to happen to Bud, if we actually find Chayne?" asks Jessica as her and Vel arrive on an old farm looking area an hour north of Lewisville.

"Well, if they don't kill him, I suppose they can stick him somewhere out here," jokes Vel in return.

Jessica hits him and snaps, "that's not funny!"

After she does the two of them exit the car and approach the entrance of a giant shed, nearly as big as a warehouse.

"This has to be it," declares Vel before lifting the latch on the door and pushing it open.

The inside is pitch black with a nearly unbearable animal odor, and spider webs that hang freely from the ceiling. An overly ambitious Vel is the first to find out.

After his episode, both he and Jessica use their cell phones to navigate around the dark shed. There are tools, barrels, and bales of hay positioned in different areas around a large fence like structure. It's purpose seems to be solely for blocking access to the in the middle of the room, or so Vel thinks. When he climbs on top of the barely seven foot wall Jessica frantically screams for him to get down, alerting him of something moving inside! Startled Vel falls off the wall, luckily landing back in front of Jessica.

"What was that for!?" he asks, his leg now thriving in pain.

"Look closely," she says, signaling for him to be quiet as well.

Initially everything grows silent, followed by the sound of charging grunts!

"Hogs!" shouts Vel after seeing one of the beasts dart through the shadows.

They seem to be circling something in the middle of the rink like setup, a stationary source of entertainment of some sort. Each one of the hogs, their number approaching double figures, take turns storming the post, viciously aiming their tusks in the general direction. The exact moment that Jessica yells aloud that she's found the light switch, another cries out in agony!

The sight is horrifying and inhumane to put it mildly, seeing Chayne chained to a bolted high chair in the middle of the rink, surrounded by a hoard of rampaging hogs. He's been badly beaten, and his pants are shredded, exposing his bloody leg wounds caused by the beasts. After mustering the strength to stand again fully, after what she has seen, Jessica proclaims the obvious, "he's been left here to die."

Vel stands mortified as well but abruptly shakes out of it responding, "and if Bud hadn't told us where he was, then he just might have."

Now they had to find a distraction that could afford them the time to snatch Chayne, time that was no longer on their side. The small bits of sunlight beginning to splash into the large windows of the warehouse cause both Vel and Jessica to look at each other even more unnerved, as the day of the championship has arrived!

Drivers are scheduled to be at the NSPCR's Championship Course, The Grand Turbine, in Dallas an hour in advance of the eleven o'clock start time. The dangers of the race come in the same form of the Turbine Seven, except this was no simulation. There has never been a repeat champion, or even a second place finish from a previous winner. After outing Sheriff Henderson as the main culprit in his kidnapping, Chayne describes to Vel and Jessica, that he believes this to be a continuation of that corrupt system. In a blink of an eye Jessica is on her laptop, requesting the names and searching each of the databases of the professional leagues ranked just above the circuit in stature. As she'd thought, she finds that none of the previous NSPCR Champions had moved on to the professional leagues as advertised, ever!

The findings hit Chayne and Vel like a bomb, their entire pursuit seeming all for naught. There's also no sight of the drivers in any post racing careers either, causing each of them to regain a firm hold on the seriousness of the situation. After Chayne expresses his concerns of dealing with a corrupt officer, especially as high ranking as the sheriff, Jessica suggests, "I'll have my dad send over one of his personal private investigators, we'll at least be able to trust him that's for sure."

"No!" yells Vel startling both Chayne and Jessica.

Returning to his stoic demeanor he declares calmly, "we have to get him back first."

"Vel we can't get into a war with law enforcement," warns Jessica.

After listening to their exchange, a light bulb goes off in Chayne's head.

Although bruised and aching he confidently declares, "but we can get into a race, and win. Hurry, I think I have an idea."

Just before they arrive at the stadium Chayne announces, "Sheriff won't be expecting me to show up, not by a long shot," gritting his teeth as he seethes over a chance at revenge.

"Okay so now you can finally tell me about the truck," inquires Vel, exposing his secret fascination with his notorious Ford Raptor.

Looking almost annoyed by the mere mention of it Chayne divulges, "oh you mean Shark Tooth? Yeah, sheriff made sure we took a trip by the crusher, for a last look before they dumped me off."

Unable to figure a decent response Vel simply states, "oh that sucks," seconds after of which Chayne defiantly retorts, "not as much as this will for him."

As he expects, Sheriff Henderson has had him replaced with another young driver, none other than Bud Sanders. When a stunned Vel tries to intervene Chayne restrains him. He warns, "trust me man, you don't know what it's like to be under his control," for the moment preferring to stay off of the sheriff's radar. Jessica sneaks off anyway, taking a winding path back to Bud. When he notices her, he promptly warns her to leave.

"You know you don't have to do this for him," she says.

The younger boy snatches his face away, but not before she sees his blackened eye. Though hesitant he speaks defiantly saying, "you don't know what I have to do. I wouldn't be here if I didn't have to be." Jessica takes one long final look at the boy, empathizing with his feeling of total helplessness, before she hears her name called in the distance.

For all of the trouble that he's put himself and Jessica through, in finding Chayne and making it to the race in time for the start, Vel would find out that there has been one final attempt to prevent his emergence as champion. Soon he is informed of another provision in the rules stipulating all participants mandatory presence, at the exact time requested for the championship final. That means at fifteen minutes after ten, which it was, the circuit commission would retain the right to allow or dismiss participants as they wished. Adding further insult to injury, a venomous note would be left in Vel's assigned pit area reading, "and at the end of the day, blacks and time will always be like oil and water," signed with the initials S.H. It isn't beyond any of them, with Sheriff Henderson garnering so much control over the circuit, that he would be behind such move, or insidious racial slur. It also isn't lost upon the group that the prideful sheriff would be unprepared for their next move in response.

Ch.16: Two Champions

Returning from a prolonged trip to the restroom Grandpa Charles finds Vel, Jessica, and to his surprise Chayne, near the pit area. Even he is surprised and in disbelief over Vel's potential disqualification.

"I had a bad feeling about this, had me in the restroom all morning," he says.

"Grandpa a young lady is standing right here!" yells Vel, easily irritable at this point.

After the tension quells Chayne eventually asks, "so how about it, you down to drive in my spot?"

Despite everyone's eyes growing wide upon his question being asked, the only other registered driver in the group was Vel.

"But how if I'm already disqualified?" asks Vel, still just as curious as everyone else.

"Champions Rule," responds Chayne, citing the open invitation to all previous champions.

It makes their criminal mystery that much more perplexing, why more past my winners have never come close to repeating, or even being competitive.

Chayne then expounds, "past winners get an invite that supersedes every circuit rule, and your car in my starting spot should work as an injury waiver for anybody that asks."

Fortunately Chayne is right, his pit area has been reserved and blocked off with curtains and red ropes, Sheriff Henderson having informed everyone that the first place leader has been scratched from the event. More sickening, he lists health reasons as the determining factor, not that he would be any less sick once the curtains were removed. While the circuit officials are performing the final track test, the group cunningly makes the move, transferring the Ford Escort into position. Just before the drivers are ready to make their appearances, the announcement is made. Over the intercom the stadium announcer reveals, "ladies and gentlemen we have a last minute update from the pit of the NSPCR defending champion. Now representing the Champions Pit, replacing Chayne Chambers and the Ford Raptor Shark Tooth, is the riveting Ford Escort known as Black Velvet!"

Surprisingly the stadium full of people roar in excitement, in hopes of seeing the incredible car, and driver, that are quickly becoming racing celebrities. Not everyone is as thrilled for him though, mainly Sheriff Henderson. He too has shocked everyone with his daylight emergence, especially Bud Sanders who looks petrified as the steaming sheriff cuts a menacing glance in his direction. After stalling to delay the race for as long as he can, circuit officials finally threaten to disqualify his drivers from the event. When the officials try again to get things under way, they are unceremoniously interrupted for a second time!

Again it is Sheriff Henderson's doing, but this time it's not him interrupting. That would happen to be what feels like a small army brigade of vehicles, all of them which are to replace his entire team of drivers! To make sure no one else says a word he puts on his badge and hat for reassurance, actually gaining the desired effect. Everyone, both officials and onlookers, watches in jaw dropping silence, if not complete awe. The car chosen to replace the pitiful looking Bud Sanders is a familiar foe to Vel, the canary colored Porsche 911. He's followed by vehicles that surely look against circuit standard, but at this point all bets are considered off. The Porsche is joined by two other cars personally requested by the conniving sheriff, a Dodge Charger 5.7 Liter AWD(All-Wheel Drive), and a Ford Sedan Police Interceptor. As soon as they join the other vehicles on the track the race begins!

In spite of the competition's speed, the first mile plays out like a high speed police chase, with Vel leading by a half car length over the sheriff's two cruisers and the Porsche. Intimidation plays a major part, as an obstacle for most of the field who have chosen to yield for the three cars working in tandem.

Another team's driver, in a Nissan, is the first to openly object to their coordinated effort to dominate the race. He dangerously swerves his bigger vehicle in front of the Sedan to break the car's formation! What he gets instead serves as a warning for the rest of the field, until the next driver is courageous enough to try them.

As the Nissan's driver completes his move he looks in his rearview, smiling at his cut off competition. Before he can turn around fully, the Dodge Charger swerves in front of him and slams on the brakes! The front of the Nissan is abruptly smashed to pieces, while the Charger resumes the race. Vel has somehow managed to maintain his lead pretty comfortably on the field, despite not having Einstein this time to combat the elements. With the distraction though, the only person still within ample striking distance is his lemon colored foe. Just like their last duel, the Porsche's driver handles the car like a defensive wizard, executing sharp counters to every attempt from Vel to thwart his surge! It's rare that audiences are treated with two competitors handling curves while both doing speeds of 100+ miles per hour, but here they had just that, with Vel and the Porsche both refusing to relent! Not alone, the two are soon rejoined by the Sedan and the partially wrecked Charger, still up to their tricks.

"Black Velvet, you're under arrest!" one of them screams over their police loudspeaker. It doesn't take long for the other to follow suit concurring, "yeah Johnny stop resisting!" Normally unmoved by the competition's antics, Vel blinks, then hesitates, allowing the Porsche to capitalize on his momentary loss of focus and take the lead! By the time another opening arrives to change positions, the Charger and Sedan have fully caught him and are threatening to bump him back into fourth place. When Vel tries to prevent their next maneuver by dodging left, the Charger ignores the dangers and cuts him off! Rather than crashing or spinning out Vel is forced into tapping the brakes. However they don't seem interested in simply halting Vel's progress momentarily, they're aiming to end his race early!

Next they coordinate an attempt that will leave the Charger out to dry as a willing sacrifice for the Porsche and Sedan, although with unwanted results. When the Charger falls behind the Sedan and hits it's brakes in front of Vel, another Ford slams it into the wall! Before a pile up can follow a caution is thought to have been called pausing the race. Luckily Vel has kept the Sedan and Porsche in his sights, because for the championship the NSPCR has decided against the use of stoppages, for any reason. At least seven lengths behind the leaders with only half of the race to go, Vel is dead set on making a comeback, not a restart.

He would have his wish, and then some, when upon entering another leg of the race the temperature drops drastically and his windows begin to frost. Unexpectedly, and beyond dangerous even for circuit standards, the road has been made completely hazardous with sheets of ice! Just as with the two cars in front of him, Vel hits the ice, sliding uncontrollably at 80 miles per hour! Unable to regain control in time, the driver of the Porsche 911 assures that the circuits infamous secret continues, of not having top finishes from past champions. The Porsche and Sedan ricochet off of each other, pin balling into and off of the wall, before the exotic yellow car instantly goes airborne! It was like there was a ramp there, the way the car projects through the air, then spirals onto it's backside,instantly marking the end of its race. That leaves the Sedan, positioned three lengths ahead of Vel, as his main source of competition. The remaining cars in the field proceed to jockey for position as the race enters it's final leg, surely hot enough for sizzling finish.

Into a volcanic area called the Devil's Pit, another championship addition, arrives each competitor, the targets of scolding balls of fire! It nearly plays out like a right of passage, how the artillery protruding from the ground takes aim at the racers as they enter the new territory, easily picking off those that become frozen in their trepidation. Seeing each of them burst into flames, tells Vel that he is a part of a very different game indeed, one in which he must race against death itself. Vel wouldn't be spooked though, or else wind up deep fried like other lesser drivers, as Black Velvet dodges left and right, weaving through the inferno. He makes it through to the finishing straightaway with the Ford Escort only adding to it's growing mystique.

Shock and awe are the only two words that can describe each spectators face in reaction to Black Velvet emerging from a volcano like tunnel, carrying with it a hood full of fiery red rocks! Even when the fire goes out the entire vehicle is left smoldering, but to his surprise, the driver of the Police Interceptor has somehow kept going with the entire top of his car on fire! The blazing Sedan whips in both directions attempting to blow out the furnace, but to no apparent success, and with no caution stoppage in sight. Even if he were to cross the finish line, marked off about only two hundred meters away, his car would inevitably be incinerated from the furnace.

Indeed, Johnny Velvet had come to another crossroads in his life. Again, he was faced with the ultimate decision, to go for sacrifice or victory. Something was different about this time though, about him. His view of the world had dramatically been altered, since his first bike or car, or street race for that matter. This time his pursuit of victory was more than just an amateur endeavor leaving him happy to get his feet wet, this was personal. He would be reminded of that with one hundred meters to go, finding Jessica's face in the audience. Even more heart clinching, she's has Grandma Thelma with her! It's the first time that she's ever been to one of Vel's races.

Trailing by three car lengths with fifty meters to go though, and the Sedan being a ticking time bomb, Vel has to make a move, and he chooses to go for it all. Reminiscent of the night of his first major street race, a light rain begins to drop, just enough to soften the ground beneath them, but not nearly strong enough to quell the Sedan's fire, or speed. In the memory of his mentor Mr. Wallace Vel declares firmly, "not today," then begins a valiant finishing maneuver. Showing no fear or hesitation he pulls the steering wheel with all of his body weight behind him, forcing the car into a sideways turning motion! As the car turns it's momentum picks up greatly, carrying it side by side with the Sedan. The impact of the move, leaving them bumper to tail light, stunningly showers the burning car with dirt and mud as both cars cross the finish line!

Johnny Velvet had done the ultimate, sacrificing his lust for victory, to once again help protect a fellow driver. Again he had ignored what would be certainly unfavorable consequences, a stinging humility to be brought on by defeat. In the face of such adversity, with his family watching, he had acted with the integrity of a champion, and with the skill of one too. It turns out that the Scandinavian Flick had come in handy after all, giving him his only hope for a photo finish to the race. The audience cheers wildly, continuing to do so long after the other drivers have completed the track, when the announcement is made.

After a close review, and a series of objections, the winner of the NSPCR Circuit Championship is announced over the stadium intercom, being none other than Black Velvet! Another explosion of cheers takes place from the crowd immediately after, while Grandpa Charles, Vel, and Chayne chaotically embrace each other in victory lane. Two champions, and a handy old man to boot, had done the improbable, but not without a little assistance from another unlikely source. Bud Sanders, looking more beat up and bandaged than before, also joins the group in their celebration, of course after admitting to being the random Ford that wrecked the Charger. All of them get a kick out his retelling of the wreck, and an even bigger boost of adrenaline when superior law enforcement shows up and takes a temper tantrum throwing Sheriff Henderson into custody! Now the only thing left for Vel was to bring down the two most important women in his tremendous young life.

Vel looks up in the stands with a smile bright enough to make the sun envious, pure joy and exoneration manifested into one valiant moment. Grandma Thelma gives him a proud smile in return, blowing a kiss to her grandson, before he signals for her he join the group. Only a few seconds later he stops celebrating altogether. Nothing can explain to him what he sees, or doesn't see, desperately turning his head back and forth as he scans the crowd to find that Jessica Hillsbury isn't there. He gets it though, that all this time he had to win for himself, with or without others in his corner. At least for the time being, he would gracefully accept the fact, that Black Velvet, and all that it encompasses, might have inspired her to do the same.

Ch.17: Finding Silver

In the months to follow Vel would join Chayne in helping him prepare for upcoming pro racing tryouts. The two champions would push each other, and their cars, to the physical limits in anticipation of a grueling entry process, and a field of drivers that were even tougher. Only past champions from registered circuits were allowed, but a one year age difference would make Chayne eligible an entire year earlier than Vel. It was something akin to the draft rules of a few other professional sports, and so Vel would humbly take his position as Chayne's training partner. Besides, there was nothing that he enjoyed more than leaving his rival in the dust every chance that he could.

Obviously, with both of them being so ultra competitive, they were bound to bump heads at some point. The day that Chayne finds out that he's been passed over sets up a perfect storm for the boy's falling out. After spending the entire previous day moving his stuff out of his grandparents home, into an apartment with Chayne, Vel finds himself totally exhausted. He finally falls asleep on the couch, not awaking until the next day. Unfortunately for Chayne's only crew help, by the time he realizes that he has missed the qualifier, Chayne is storming back inside with the bad news! After their argument Vel moves back in with his grandparents.

Hours later it's just Vel by himself, left in his same old room, in the same old house.

"Hey my sweet champion, the food is just about ready," chimes Grandma Thelma's loving voice from the hallway, to which there is no response. She follows up by asking, "so is this how it feels to finally be a champion, the Black Velvet?"

Unable to answer her directly Vel stares blankly at the ceiling before sitting up. When he looks at her, his eyes hold the weight of a largely mysterious, and often times brutal, world.

"I don't know," he replies solemnly.

Before leaving him to his thoughts Grandma Thelma reveals, "oh, and you got a phone call today while you were out, they left a voicemail."

Given a time and address to show up in less than thirty minutes, Vel grabs his jacket and zips from the house!

Thirty minutes prior Jessica, whom had been staying in a hotel in the area, has just finished packing her bags and is ready to leave town for good. The last item, which she puts into her purse, is a small heart framed picture of Vel from graduation. Before she closes her purse a final teardrop falls inside. Promptly after her cell phone rings, and it's her father, calling to inform her on the status of one of their previous agreements.

He confirms, "it's been done princess, and I want you to know that I'll always love you no matter what. You always have tried your best, to protect others."

Afterwards she grabs her keys and rushes out the door, leaving her purse and phone behind.

Outside, her father has delivered an unfathomable gift of his endearing affection, a completely rebuilt Chevy Camaro ZL1! Engraved in the driver side head rest is the nickname, "Silver." When she gets inside and starts it, the real race has just begun. A polished black Escort pulls up next to her, Vel, at the same time that a hulking Ford Raptor pulls up on the opposite side.

Confirming the look of wonder in Jessica's eyes Vel yells aloud, "yeah your dad pulled some real strings to bring Chayne's truck back from the dead!"

Chayne, feeling as cool as he can be, back inside of his newly renovated racing monster, fixes his sunglasses in the mirror then chimes in jokingly, "yeah, but I'll have to get use to Shark Tooth being all neon greenish though."

"Yeah sorry about that," agrees a giggling Jessica, accepting the mishap of her father as her own.

"Did you--," begins Chayne, before Jessica abruptly shakes her head yes.

"Man you're right Velvet, she's not too bad," he says before revving Shark Tooth loudly.

"How about we get this sixty roll going!?" urges Vel, ready to test his friends once again, for old times.

Jessica confidently agrees, "let's do it, Black Velvet" then smashes her foot on the gas!

www.ingramcontent.com/pod-product-compliance
Lightning Source LLC
La Vergne TN
LVHW010606160826
845677LV00013B/3273

* 9 7 9 8 3 6 7 3 0 0 4 8 2 *